Since Drew

J. Nathan

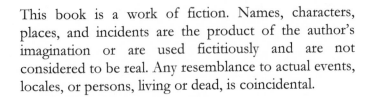

This book is a work of fiction. Names, characters, places, and incidents are the product of the author's imagination or are used fictitiously and are not considered to be real. Any resemblance to actual events, locales, or persons, living or dead, is coincidental.

Edited by Stephanie Elliot

Cover Design by RBA Designs
Cover Photo © Vishstudio|Andrei Vishnyakov via Dreamstime.com

Manufactured in the United States of America

Second Edition May 2015

ISBN-13: 978-1508875420 (Print edition only)
ISBN-10: 1508875421 (Print edition only)

*For my husband and son, who
share me with this big dream of mine.*

PROLOGUE

I pushed back the blonde strands that escaped my ponytail and stuck to my sweaty face. My sneakers clapped off the pavement in even successions. My pace was good. Breathing controlled. Heart rate just right.

Late night jogging along the coast always gave me the jolt of adrenaline I needed before a big race. And since only one spot remained on the Olympic team, tomorrow's qualifying race was the mother of all races. It's what I trained for. It's what I worked for. It's what I thought about every hour of every day for as long as I could remember.

It was the first week of May. And though beachgoers had already descended upon Wilmington, the road remained deserted. Just the way I liked it. I'd purposely left my phone at home so my feet on the pavement and the waves crashing on the shore could serenade me, soothing me like nothing else.

I began the slight uphill incline, focusing all my attention on winning the gold. Not my parents thousands of miles away on their latest crusade. Not my final exams—which if I hoped to graduate from UNC at the end of the month, I probably should've gotten my ass home to hit the books. And not my ex who dumped me right after spring break for someone not nearly as wonderful as me—*just saying*. But it didn't stop me from mentally plotting a painful demise. One that included him contracting an incurable STD after discovering the tramp was underage and her parents were pressing charges. *Again. Just saying.*

With a wide grin and proverbial pat on the back, I picked up speed.

Lights from a vehicle approaching from behind lit up the upcoming bend in the road. Now I could actually see the guardrail to my right and the fierce waves crashing down below. Had I not checked the weather, I would've assumed a storm approached. And there was nothing, except running, that I loved more than a storm. The violent winds. Dark clouds. Mighty waves. Pitter-patter off the window panes. Pure serenity.

The vehicle's tires crunched over the sandy pavement as it neared, tearing my attention back to the road. My eyes shifted, only to be blinded by headlights. The car was close. Too close. My only hope was that the driver had seen me.

They hadn't.

My feet ripped out from beneath me. Pain tore through me as my body flipped over the car with unfathomable speed. My limbs shot out, contorting in unnatural positions as I slammed into the unforgiving concrete.

Then nothing.
Nothing but blackness.

CHAPTER ONE

Pain pounded through my body like a jackhammer let loose on a slab of cement. Everything felt fuzzy. Distant. Silent. *Eerily* silent. Nothingness filled the void surrounding me. Not the ocean. Not a siren signifying help. Not my own desperate screams lost in the darkness.

I needed to get up. I needed to get home. I needed to open my eyes. But they were stuck. Thick crust rendered them incapable. Was it tears? Blood? Something else? I tried again, feeling the top lashes wrench free from the bottom as my eyelids split apart. Blinding light pierced my retinas, forcing them shut.

I drew a deep breath, prepared this time for the intrusion. Sunlight infiltrated the stark white hospital room where I lay in a bed. A curtain cocooned me on my left. A drip bag and the monitors attached to my body sat on my right. My eyes shot down to the white blanket covering my body. Something was wrong with me. Something was *seriously* wrong with me.

My breath hitched.

Fear grabbed hold of me.

My heart thumped harder.

My legs.

I couldn't move my legs.

As if I'd removed ear protectors, sounds whooshed through my head like a vacuum, rattling my ear drums. Noisy monitors beeped around me. Nurses shuffled by my open door. The voice on the hallway PA requested a doctor on the second floor.

But the only thing that mattered, the only thing that had the power to make or break me, lay underneath the covers.

Terrified, I grabbed hold of the blanket, bunching it in my hands until I worked up the nerve to actually go through with it. I inhaled a deep breath and yanked it off.

Oh. My. God.

A bulky cast covered my right leg from my knee to my ankle. A pillow elevated my left knee, which was stabilized with a brace and surrounded by ice packs. Sweat beaded on my hairline. Numbness washed over me. Too many thoughts bombarded my mind at once. I wasn't drunk, but my head spun as though I were. I buried my face in my palms, feeling a bandage covering my right cheek.

"*Fuuuuuck*," I roared into my hands.

The curtain to my left ripped open.

I stilled, knowing whoever just overheard my breakdown stood waiting for me to work it out.

Fat chance of that.

But I was Andi Parker. And I could fake it like no one's business.

I sucked a deep breath in through my nose, pulling it together long enough to face whoever waited. Dropping my hands, I let my head fall to the left.

A dark-haired stranger lounging on the opposite bed grinned. "You're up."

My tongue stuck to the roof of my mouth as I pushed the words out. "Tell me I'm dead."

His dark brows scrunched as he shook his head. "Nope."

"Is this a dream?"

His lips slid into a slow cocky grin. "It's definitely not the first time I've heard that one."

"A nightmare then?"

Amused, he swung his legs off the side of the bed and sat facing me. "If waking up next to a hot guy constitutes nightmare for you, I guess there's a first time for everything."

My eyes drifted over his white T-shirt, khaki cargo shorts, and bare feet. Was he a patient? "Do you always refer to yourself as hot?" God, my voice was weak.

He threw his head back and laughed. There was something soothingly warm about his raspy laugh. Something calming. Something ethereal.

"Who are you?"

He pointed to himself like I'd asked a crazy question. "Me?"

I nodded my throbbing head.

"Well, it seems as though having a name like Andi confused admissions. I'm your roommate Drew."

Roommate? I stared blankly at this guy who couldn't be much older than me, perusing his slightly tanned face and rosy cheeks. His perfect nose and scarlet lips. He didn't look sick. My eyes lowered to his muscular arms. His strong hands gripping the edge of the bed. His well-defined thigh muscles and calves dangling off the side of the bed. He certainly didn't look hurt.

"When the nurses took one look at you…"

My eyes shot up to his face. "What?"

His eyes drifted over my hospital gown. "Let's just say, on top of it being against hospital policy to have us in the same room, they're pretty concerned we'll..." His voice drifted off, purposely prolonging the suspense.

Seriously? Did I look like I needed suspense in my life? I was a mess. "We'll what?"

His big emerald eyes jumped to mine as his lips twitched wildly. "Go at it like rabbits."

Under normal circumstances, I would've laughed, finding him a little charming—okay, a lot charming. But in that moment, with my entire future hanging in the balance, I just needed to know one thing. "What's wrong with me?"

He tilted his head, those pretty eyes boring into mine. "The nurses said you broke your leg and tore your ACL."

A whoosh of air punched out of my lungs as the stark realization slammed into me like an eighteen-wheeler. I squeezed my eyes shut, keeping any tears that dared to creep to the surface at bay.

I'd never stand on that platform.

I'd never wear a medal around my neck.

I'd never hear the national anthem played as American fans looked on with pride.

I'd. Never. Run. Again.

I pressed my palms into my eyes, pushing everything away. The heartbreaking thoughts. The tears prickling the backs of my eyes. The monotonous pounding in my head. The intense need to throw myself out the nearest window. My luck I'd be on the first floor.

This was the moment. The moment I realized everything I'd worked for my entire life had just been ripped away from me.

The twisting ache in my stomach tightened. If I were standing, I would've keeled over. It hurt. It hurt like hell. But I wouldn't cry. Andi Parker didn't cry. She also didn't refer to herself in the third-person. But here she sat doing just that. Again.

Mother-effer.

I dropped my hands and steeled myself.

"I told the doctor I'd get him when you woke up." Drew stood from his bed, taller and broader than I expected. If I hadn't just been delivered a life-shattering blow, I might've taken a moment to admire the way his chest filled out his T-shirt or the way his shorts hung low on his hips.

"How long have I been out?" I could barely hear the sound of my own voice. I was under water and sinking quickly.

"They pumped you with some heavy pain meds. You've been in and out for a couple days."

A couple days?

Drew shot me a regrettable frown as he made his way to the door and disappeared into the hallway.

Within seconds, a doctor in a white coat stepped through the doorway with Drew on his heels. "Good morning. I'm Doctor Evans." His tall body stopped at my bedside, towering over me. "You had quite an accident."

"Will I be able to run again?" My voice cracked with emotion.

"Well, you fractured your tibia and fibula in your right leg and needed open reduction and internal fixation surgery. You suffered a complete tear of your ACL in your left knee which we also repaired."

My voice became firmer. "Will I be able to run again?"

"The ACL will be fine once we get the physical therapist up here to help you regain movement. After that, the goal is to achieve and maintain full knee extension and increase muscle function in your quadriceps."

I felt myself slipping as I sat dazed by the information overload and his reluctance to answer my question.

"Thanks to all the hardware in your right leg, prognosis for a full recovery is high." He crossed his arms. "As for running?"

I held my breath.

"You'll be non-weight bearing for quite some time."

All the air rushed out of me.

There was no way, in even four years when the next Olympics rolled around, I'd be able to compete at the level I'd been at. And then, there'd be younger and faster runners who'd surpass me.

"On top of that," Doctor Evans' voice broke through my spiraling thoughts. "You suffered brain swelling—clinically referred to as cerebral edema."

And the hits just keep on coming.

"I know this is probably a lot to take in right now."

Ya think?

"From what the EMTs said when they brought you in…" He tipped his head thoughtfully. "You were extremely lucky to have survived the accident."

I glanced to Drew sitting on the edge of his bed, his lips twisting regrettably.

"On a scale of one to ten, what's your pain level?" Doctor Evans asked.

I wanted to ask which pain he referred to. The physical or emotional? "Five."

He slipped a flashlight from his coat pocket and shined it into my eyes. "How's the head feeling?"

"Like I had a killer night out with friends."

Drew snickered as Doctor Evans stared into my eyes. "So, you feel hung over?"

"More like I did too many shots, went home with a guy I didn't know, and let him do dirty things to me that I can't remember."

Drew choked out a laugh.

Doctor Evans lowered his light wearing a slight smirk. "Tell you what. I'll have the nurses get you something for that head."

"Thanks."

He tucked the flashlight back into his pocket. "Smart move carrying your license. We were able to get your parents on the phone long enough to get their consent to operate before losing the connection."

"I'm lucky you got them at all. They're off the coast of Antarctica."

"Oh?"

"Stopping whale hunters," I explained, like it was the most normal thing in the world—though I knew it was the complete opposite. "They usually can't be reached out there."

He crossed his arms. "Any other relatives we can contact for you?"

"No."

"Friends?"

I nodded. "I can call my best friend."

"That must be the young woman who's been causing quite a scene in the waiting room."

I closed my eyes on a slight nod. "That would be Logan."

"Is she your roommate?"

I shook my head. "I live alone."

A look of disappointment passed over Doctor Evans' features, crinkling the aging skin around his eyes.

"What?"

"I'd have a difficult enough time discharging you if it was just limited mobility in your legs. But with cerebral edema and knowing no one's at home to assist you..." He shook his head. "I won't discharge you. Not yet anyway."

I should've felt angry. Alone. Devastated that he planned to keep me a prisoner. But he was right. How would I ever be able to maneuver around my tiny condo alone? And even if Logan left her sorority house to stay with me, I'd still be in a wheelchair which wouldn't fit down my narrow hallway.

"I've got to finish my rounds, but I'll send a nurse in with those meds. And your friend, *if* she's calmed down." Doctor Evans shot me a small smile before he headed out the door.

"So, hot guy? Dirty things?" Drew kicked up his bare feet and linked his hands behind his head, settling back onto his bed. "Why do I get the feeling it was me you were referring to?"

My eyes drifted to his penetrating eyes. All that was missing was the baseball hat pulled down low. "Nope. Not my type."

He leveled me with a skeptical look.

"I'm totally into blondes with blue eyes." Sarcasm beat wallowing in self-pity. Being angry at the world. Crying until I was out of tears. I was a fighter. A devastated fighter, but a fighter nonetheless.

Drew stifled a grin as he jumped to his feet and headed to the door. "I'll go make sure your friend's not freaking out."

Within minutes, Logan burst through my door with her arms flailing. "Oh, thank God."

Anyone witnessing the scene might've assumed we were sisters. Both natural blondes with blue eyes. But our similarities stopped there. I was tall, skinny, and painstakingly average while Logan was petite, curvy, and drop-dead beautiful.

She shook the entire bed as she dropped down beside me and threw her arms around me, holding on for dear life. "Are you okay?"

"Do I look okay?" I mumbled into her shoulder.

She pulled back, her eyes drifting down to my legs. That's when I noticed tears running down her cheeks. "The Olympics?"

I shook my head.

She lifted her hand to the bandage on my cheek. "Oh, honey. I'm so sorry."

I nodded, stopping my own tears from leaking out.

"If you weren't all broken and bruised, I'd kick your ass for jogging alone in the middle of the night, you know that, right?" She wiped her eyes, fixing her smudged mascara in the process.

"I know."

"But I love you and will do whatever you need me to do," she assured me.

I managed something resembling a smile. "I know that, too."

That was the last thing I remembered before sleep pulled me under and despair filled my dreams.

CHAPTER TWO

I hung up the phone, unable to reach my parents yet again. Sure, I'd been enduring their disappearing act since freshmen year in high school. But seriously? Right now I needed my mommy and daddy.

I often wondered if it was my fault. If I'd made it too easy for them to just pick up and take off across the globe on one of their crazy adventures. If knowing I was at home getting good grades, focusing on track, and never giving them a reason to worry had backfired on me. Maybe if I'd thrown the occasional party, been caught sneaking out to meet a guy, or come home drunk off my ass, it would've given them cause to rethink their getaways. But I hadn't. So there I sat. Alone once again.

I grabbed the remote and flipped on the small flat screen across from my bed. My head was a tenuous place to be. I needed a distraction to keep me out of it. To keep me from dwelling on my loneliness, my misery, my shattered dreams. To keep me sane.

"Knock. Knock."

My eyes flashed to the doorway where a welcome distraction stood in faded jeans, a navy T-shirt, and a grin. He wasn't there when I woke the previous night or that morning. "You're up early."

Drew shrugged. "Yeah, I couldn't really sleep without your cute little snoring next to me."

My eyes flared. "I don't snore."

"Yes, you do."

My forehead creased. "Wait. Where'd you sleep?"

"Now that you're awake, they kicked my sorry ass out of here."

"I had no idea."

He gripped the doorframe, teetering between the hallway and my room. "Does that mean you wanted me to stay?" His voice had dropped to a sexy tenor.

"Don't get crazy now." My lips kicked up on one side, an oddity given my current situation. "Do they let all patients roam the halls here or just you?"

Drew stepped inside. "It's not a jail."

I glanced down at my legs. "Sure feels that way."

His eyes examined my cast and brace as he dropped into the chair beside me. The nurse who'd changed the bandage on my cheek found me a pair of shorts and a white T-shirt with the hospital logo. Anything beat a hospital gown. Drew must've felt the same since I hadn't seen him in one either. "Yeah. Sucks to be you."

"Empathetic much?"

He flashed what I assumed to be his panty-melter grin. Nope. It was *definitely* his panty-melter grin. "I like the booty shorts."

Feeling vulnerable under his gaze, my traitorous cheeks heated.

"You gonna let me be the first to sign the cast?"

I cocked me head. "Does anyone over the age of ten actually do that?"

He shrugged as he pulled open the bedside drawer and rummaged through it.

"Forget something?"

"Like what?"

"Oh, I don't know. Clothes, snacks, condoms."

His hand froze as his eyes cut to mine. "That an invitation?"

"What? God, no." I shouldn't have sounded so repulsed, because really, with his good looks, amazing body, and quick wit, Drew seemed to be the total package. "You haven't even told me why you're here. It might be some contagious STD."

He continued rummaging through the drawer with a knowing smirk.

"No, seriously. Why is it that you've got the run of this place?" I asked.

He pulled a pen from the drawer. "I'm sick. They take pity on the ill."

I waited for him to elaborate, to shed some light on the circumstances that brought him to this place, a place no healthy person remained longer than a brief visit. But instead of indulging me, he crouched at my ankle and attempted to write on my cast.

Too bad for him. I didn't back down that easily. "So, how long have you been here?"

He didn't look up. "Not much longer than you."

"Yet here you are seemingly fine."

"Oh, I'm far from fine." He remained focused on the spot on my cast, working the pen over the bumpy plaster. "They're just trying to figure out what's wrong with me. You know, running tests."

"What kind of tests?"

Those pretty green eyes, encased by thick dark lashes, flashed up. They were cloudy. Unamused. Uncomfortable. Was his prognosis something serious? More serious than he let on? "Speaking of tests…" He jumped to his feet. "I've got another one in a few minutes. They're probably looking for me." He tossed the pen on my tray table. "This doesn't work anyway."

He disappeared into the hallway, leaving me wondering what I'd said to cause him to rush out so quickly.

* * *

I switched off the afternoon talk show I wasn't really watching. I'd had a tough morning. The visiting physical therapist stopped by and gave my knee an agonizing stretch. Thankfully, the pain meds helped with my soreness and discomfort. Unfortunately, they didn't ease the pain brought on by my coach's phone call.

I closed my eyes, desperately needing to sleep. Needing to forget his call. Needing to ignore the fact that while unconscious, Marley Edwards slipped into my spot. She'd be outfitted in red, white, and blue. She'd be entering with team USA while onlookers cheered with their flags waving. She'd be in contention for the medal.

"Ms. Parker?"

My eyes popped open. A police officer filled the doorway. Given his large frame, menacing qualities, and the fact that he wasn't carrying a 1980's boom box ready to slip on some cheesy techno music and rip off his uniform, Logan hadn't sent me a stripper.

"I'm Officer Roy." He walked inside, eyeing the chair beside my bed. "Mind if I sit?" I shook my head as he lowered himself into it, pulling out a small notepad. "I just need to ask you a few questions."

"Okay."

"Do you have any recollection of what happened the night of your accident?"

My head fell back into the pillow as my thoughts transported me. "I was out for a run." I zoned in on a chipped piece of plaster on the ceiling, remembering the slapping of my sneakers on the concrete. The fierceness of the waves. The thick salty air. "I always run on that road. It's usually deserted at that time of night." I looked to him, vigorously jotting down my words. "I heard a car approaching." Knots of unease formed in my stomach. "I glanced to the side, but all I could see were lights. Bright headlights. Before I even saw the car, it hit me. I blacked out and woke up here."

He stopped writing and looked up at me. "Sounds scary."

"I was unconscious for most of it. I was kind of hoping you'd be able to fill in the blanks."

He tucked the small pad into his pocket. "From what I could surmise, the driver lost control of his vehicle."

Wow. I hadn't even considered the driver. "Did he make it?"

"Barely."

"Was anyone else in the car?"

He shook his head.

"Geez."

He pulled a small card from his pocket. "If you remember anything else, even if it seems trivial, I want you to call me."

I took the card from his outstretched hand. "Okay."

He stood and walked to the door, stopping in the doorway and glancing over his shoulder. "Take care, Ms. Parker."

I looked down at my useless legs, knowing I had one hell of a road ahead. "I'll try."

Once he left, I closed my eyes. It had taken more effort than expected to recall the accident. The complete darkness. The tires crunching over the sandy pavement. The fear I felt knowing I couldn't protect myself.

"What do you say we get outta here?"

My eyes snapped open. Drew leaned casually against my door jamb. "If you hadn't noticed, I can't walk."

He eyed my legs. "So?"

I tilted my head. "You planning on carrying me? Because if so, you're gonna need a fork lift."

A sly smile crept across his lips. "For the record, I could carry your tiny body for days, soaking wet, across continents and oceans."

I eyed his short sleeves tightly gripping his impressive biceps. I didn't doubt it for a second.

"It's the damn cast." He nodded at the awful thing. "It'd take out everyone in our path." He disappeared into the hallway and returned pushing a wheelchair.

I held up my palm, stopping him from moving closer. "Thanks for the offer. But I don't really feel like going anywhere."

His forehead creased. "Why not?"

"Well, I haven't showered. I've got this ridiculous bandage on my face. And, I'm pretty miserable company."

He flipped up the chair's right leg rest. "You think any of that's going to stop me?"

The confident look in his eyes, as he abandoned the wheelchair and walked over to the side of my bed, seriously called into question my power of persuasion. He planted his hands on the mattress. It dipped under his weight.

A deep ripple rolled through my body and tiny prickles attacked my arms as his fresh scent wrapped itself around me invading all my senses.

I needed him to back up before I did something stupid, like pull him to me and go crazy on his lips. "Just because we were roommates for like a second, it doesn't mean you have to do this."

"Who said that's why I'm doing it?" Sincerity shone his eyes, *or* he was one hell of an actor. Without warning, he slipped his hands underneath me, cradling me in his arms like I weighed nothing at all. *Good God, he was strong.* Unwilling to concede and wrap my arms around his neck, they dangled limply at my sides. He twisted and set me down in the wheelchair, slipping my cast into the raised rest. "Where to?"

Except for the fleeting bout of dizziness that momentarily afflicted me, sitting upright in something other than a hospital bed felt nice. Refreshing even. "Surprise me."

"Fair enough. But I can't take you too far looking like that." His eyes trailed over my hospital shorts and T-shirt.

"Wouldn't want to embarrass you."

"*Embarrass me?* Are you kidding? The guys around here would be congratulating me. It's no easy feat getting such a honey to go out with me."

I lifted a skeptical brow.

His smug smile confirmed he had no trouble with the ladies. "So…" he mused. "A fancy restaurant's out of the question. The movies would be too uncomfortable for the poor schmuck in front of you. And a walk on the beach would mean you could actually walk—"

"Seriously? You're like the most unsympathetic person I've ever met." I couldn't decide if I was aghast by his callous statement or amused he had the balls to actually say it.

He grinned. "Oh, I sympathize. I was just stating the obvious."

I rolled my eyes. "How about some fresh air?"

His grin widened as he stepped behind the chair and wheeled me out of the room, careful not to slam my cast into the door jamb.

Heads turned as we made our way down the hallway. Some nurses smiled. Some did a double take. Some waved. Who could blame them? The hottest guy in the hospital was pushing me around.

When we reached the elevator, Drew spun my chair and backed me inside. It was only then I realized my room was on the fifth floor. "Are you on this floor, too?"

He shook his head as we began our descent. "Nope. Got demoted from the penthouse."

"Thanks to me?"

"Thanks to you."

The elevator doors split on the ground floor. Drew pushed me through the busy lobby, avoiding the main entrance where what looked to be a group of reporters with cameras waited outside.

"What's going on out there?"

Drew pushed me to the sliding glass doors at the side of the lobby, as far away from the front doors as we could get. "No idea."

I closed my eyes as we passed through the doors, embracing the warmth of the afternoon sunlight on my skin. I took a nice deep breath, inhaling the crisp fresh air while ridding my senses of the sterile hospital smell for the first time in days.

When I opened my eyes, an unexpected oasis surrounded the building. Pastel flower beds covered the grounds. Wood benches sat scattered in shaded areas under blooming cherry trees. And a brick walking path lined the perimeter of the freshly-cut lawn.

Drew pushed me onto the path, walking us slowly around the property.

"Are you allowed to be out here with your condition?" I asked.

"You make it sound like I should be in a bubble." It came out light-heartedly, but I wondered what really ran through that head of his.

"Should you?"

"No," he laughed.

Not one to relent easily, I kept at it. "How'd your test go? Did they find anything?"

He maneuvered me around some raised bricks. "Nope."

"Are you in any pain?"

"Not in the traditional sense of the word."

I tried reeling in the frustrated huff that escaped my lips, but I really wanted to know his deal, and he was being so evasive. "You haven't told me where you're from."

"You haven't asked."

"Seriously? It's like playing twenty-questions with you."

He snickered. "Just outside Raleigh. You?"

Up until my accident, I'd planned to travel wherever the Olympics and subsequent events took me. Not anymore. "Right here in Wilmington."

"Oh yeah? My parents' beach house is here."

"That's weird. I've never seen you around."

He remained behind me, but I could tell he shrugged his broad shoulders. "I'm usually busy in the summer. And I'm not really into the whole beach scene. Don't get me wrong. Girls in bikinis, totally my thing. But spending time with my family, not so much."

"That bad?"

"Worse."

We passed a little girl kicking a ball on the grass with her parents. Her mother wore a hospital robe and a smile, clearly longing to be home with her family.

"I heard you mention your parents," Drew said from behind. "They sound…interesting."

"That's one way of describing them."

"So, whales?" Amusement colored his tone.

I nodded. "I couldn't change them, even if I wanted to."

"So, you're not into all that stuff?"

I looked over my shoulder. Drew's eyes were trained on the path ahead. "What stuff?"

He glanced down. Our eyes met for a long moment before he spoke. "Saving the world."

I shook my head. I'd been too consumed with getting to the Olympics to save the world. Now, I just needed to save myself.

"You still in school?" he asked, taking the lead in our game of twenty-questions.

I turned around, enjoying the beauty surrounding us as we walked. "I'm supposed to graduate from UNC next month."

"No shit," he said, like it was the most interesting news he'd heard in a long time. "I'm graduating from Duke."

"Duke? That's impressive."

"Not really. They used me for my arm. I used them for their name."

"Your arm?"

"Football," he explained. "I'm a quarterback."

Of course he was. *Athletic drive*. That's what I saw in his eyes. The same look I possessed for the last eight years.

"So, you think you'll be able to walk across the stage by then?" he asked.

My brows dipped, confused by his hasty subject change. "I have no idea if I'll even be on crutches by then."

Drew parked me beside a secluded bench under one of the cherry trees covered with beautiful, pale pink flowers. He sat down beside me, turning his body to face mine. "I could push you."

My eyes jumped to his, expecting to see humor dancing in their green depths. But that's not what I found. He'd been serious "You barely even know me."

"Oh, I know you all right."

I chewed my bottom lip, unnerved by the implication of his words. "Oh, yeah?"

"Yeah."

I studied his striking features, curious as to what he could possibly know. I fanned out my hand. "By all means. Enlighten me."

He straightened his spine, prepared for the challenge. "You don't have many loyal people in your life who stick by you when you need them."

I crossed my arms as if they could somehow shield me from his candid assessment. "You know that from talking to me a couple times?"

"I know that because, since you've been here, no one's visited you except your crazy friend."

I averted my gaze, slightly embarrassed by the fact that he'd been right. I didn't have many close friends. I'd always been too busy running and training. It wasn't like track was a team sport. I spent most of my time alone. And not until that moment, not until he'd pointed it out after knowing me for a couple days, had I considered it something to be ashamed of. I mean, isn't one close friend you can trust with your life better than a bunch of quasi-friends who could turn on you at the drop of a dime? My eyes shot back to Drew's. "Logan's not crazy. She's just passionate."

His unconvinced expression caused us both to burst into laughter. "We'll agree to disagree on that one. Besides, we're talking about you. And you're determined."

My laughter ceased. "Why would you say that?"

"Your questions to the doc. About running."

I nodded. I was determined. A lot of good that did me now.

"And did I mention cute?" he asked with a sexy as sin grin. "Because you're *damn* cute."

I suppressed a smile. "Obviously."

"And modest."

"Don't forget humble," I smirked.

"And sarcastic."

We shared another laugh. It felt refreshing to actually let go of all the angst eating me up inside—at least for a little while. "You should be careful. I'm kind of needy these days. I might just take you up on your offer."

"You'd be a fool not to. Most girls would pay big money to have me with them on one of the biggest days of their life."

"Prom?"

He cocked his head, not bothering to respond. But I could tell he enjoyed our easy banter as much as I did.

"Even if I can still take my finals and graduate on time, I'm not sure you, me, and your big head will make it across the stage."

I thought he'd laugh or crack a joke, but he didn't. Something had changed. It was as if a switch snapped off, and he'd disappeared inside himself. His attention moved to the football that rolled to his feet. He reached down and picked it up, looking to the boys who'd been playing catch across the lawn. I expected him to show off his arm and toss it back to them, but he didn't. Instead, he handed it to me.

"You want me to throw it?"

He nodded.

I grabbed the ball, gripping the bumpy leather and aligning my fingertips on the lacing like my dad had shown me to do when I was his little tomboy. I drew a breath, hoping I didn't throw it like a total girl and embarrass myself. I pulled back my arm, releasing it in one quick movement. It sailed with ease though the air in a perfect spiral.

"Nice throw," Drew said, seemingly surprised the ball actually landed in the guy's hands.

"One of my many talents."

He still didn't laugh.

"What's wrong? You scared of a little competition?"

For a long time, he stayed silent, just staring out across the property watching the guys playing catch. Their throws were nowhere near as perfect as mine—of course. But they were having fun. Laughing and joking around. Dodging around each other when they had the ball. Cheering when they scored an imaginary touchdown.

"I'm supposed to be drafted to the pros." Drew's deep voice startled me.

My head whipped to him. "The pros? That's amazing."

His gaze stayed locked on the guys. "That's what everyone keeps telling me. But no one's really asked if it's what I want to do."

I paused, unsure if he wanted me to ask or not. "Do you?"

He shrugged.

"I can't imagine playing a sport and not wanting to reach the pinnacle of it."

"Oh, believe me. It happens." No humor laced his voice.

I nodded, though I didn't understand. Our circumstances were so different. "I was supposed to make it to the Olympics. The qualifying round was the day after my accident. And I wanted it. I wanted it so bad I could taste it." My shoulders dropped on an exhale as I stared out across the lawn. "Now I'll never have it, and I have absolutely no idea what to do with that." I looked down at the contraptions hindering my dream. I felt myself getting choked up—never having vocalized it that way before. I pushed down the brewing emotion. I needed to stay strong.

When I turned to Drew, his eyes were on me and no longer distant and distracted, but soft and concerned. "Which event?"

"Oh. Wait for it. It's good…800-meter track."

"*Fuuuuck.*" It was a mere whisper, but it said it all.

We turned at the same time and stared out at the grounds. Drew's eyes followed the guys enjoying their game of football. Playing because they loved it. Not because it was what they were supposed to do. My eyes followed patients happily strolling around with their visitors. But I knew the truth. They weren't happy. They were prisoners. Trapped in an existence they didn't ask for. One they didn't want. One they needed out of.

"I'm sorry," Drew's raspy voice offered.

I shrugged. "It's not your fault."

A young nurse appeared out of nowhere, stopping in front of us. "Andi. I need to get you back inside. Doctor Evans is doing his rounds and wants to see you."

My eyes shot to Drew.

A sad smile touched his lips. "You go. I'm kind of enjoying the fresh air. I'll stop by to see you later."

I nodded as the nurse stepped behind my chair and pushed me away from him.

CHAPTER THREE

"So tell me more about Mr. Tall, Dark, and Gorgeous."

"*Shhhh.*" My eyes shifted to the empty doorway. "My luck, he'll hear you. And that'll only inflate his already massive ego."

Logan kicked her flip-flops up onto my bed from the chair beside me. "Sweetie, if he's half as sexy as you say he is, one, an ego's to be expected. And, two, he'd love hearing I'm interested."

She was right. He would. Guys fell over themselves to be with Logan. She and Drew would make the perfect pair. And for some reason, the thought twisted my insides.

"So, what do you think he's got?"

"I have a feeling it's cancer. Maybe it's in remission. I don't know. But they don't just let someone roam the halls if they're contagious."

"That sucks," she said. "He's young, right?"

"Senior at Duke. Quarterback on their football team. And, get this. He's supposed to be drafted to the pros."

Logan's blue eyes expanded and a proven-to-win-pageants smile overtook her glossy lips.

"Oh, no, you don't. No sinking your teeth into my only friend in this place."

Logan laughed as she tapped away at her phone. "I'm sure *he* wouldn't mind my teeth anywhere near him."

I rolled my eyes. "You're probably right."

"Probably?"

I flipped her off.

"Whoa." She gazed down at her phone. "His name's Drew Slater. He's got close to fifty-thousand followers. And he's *hot*."

Slater? With all my questions, how had I not asked him that? "Let me see."

She held out her phone. The picture on his page was of him in his football uniform. *Good Lord.* If I thought he was hot in his normal clothes, there was something about him in that tight uniform that— "Put it away." I shoved her phone back at her.

"Huh?"

I shook my head. "I don't want to see anymore."

A smug smile tipped her lips. "You're welcome for bringing your stuff."

I stared at her blankly. Had I zoned out for part of our conversation?

"No, I get it," she said casually. "You wanna look at it in private when I leave."

"Ewww. No."

She unleashed a devilish laugh.

"You know I'm not into all that."

"Into all what exactly? Because if you're forgetting, we went to that sex shop together last year and I saw what you bought."

I cocked my head, letting my serious eyes speak for me. "Cyber-stalking. You know I hate that. It makes girls crazy."

"But don't you want to know what he's got?"

"If he doesn't know, I doubt any of his followers know. I'm serious Logan. Put it away. I feel funny searching him. Anything I want to know, I'll get from him."

Logan's smile faded as she tucked her phone into her handbag. "Andi? You sure it's a good idea getting chummy with someone who's not gonna stick around? You know how that tired scene plays out."

My forehead creased, suddenly uncomfortable with her concern. "I know that."

"Do you? Because whether he's drafted, or—" She lowered her voice. "Dead. He's gone."

The truth pinched deep in my gut. Yes, the Olympics were gone. Yes, my ex was gone. And, yes, for all intents and purposes, my parents were gone. But look at me. I was holding it together. "I just met the guy."

She arched her perfect brow and held me with a presumptuous gaze.

I looked away just as Drew passed by my room. "Hey," I called out.

Logan spun toward the now empty doorway. "Was that him?"

"Yeah."

She sprang to her feet and hurried into the hallway. Her blonde curls whipped left then right, before she turned toward me. "I don't see him."

"He probably didn't want to interrupt." Or he'd heard everything we'd said.

I closed my eyes as my head nestled deeper into my pillow. *Fan-freaking-tastic.*

* * *

I'd been watching a family of birds chirping outside my window all day. Scratch that. Since giving up on the assignments Logan brought from my professors.

A food server shuffled into my room, leaving behind my dinner tray. My rumbling stomach told me my hunger, which had been nonexistent since waking up in the hospital, had returned. Unfortunately, as I picked away at the dry lump of meatloaf, I knew it wasn't going to cut it.

"Did someone order a pizza?" Drew walked in carrying a pizza box.

"Ahhh. My pizza boy fantasy."

Amusement crossed his face. "You have a pizza boy fantasy?" He placed the box on the bedside table just out of my reach and pulled out a slice.

"I do now."

He flashed a knowing smile. "But you didn't yesterday?"

I shook my head, wondering if he'd mentioned yesterday because he hadn't been around *or* because he hoped I'd bring up Logan. It's what guys did. Found a way to segue into talking about her. Then none-too-subtly asked me to hook them up. It got old fast.

Drew dropped into the chair beside my bed. His eyes stayed locked on mine as he bit into his slice. "*Mmmm.* Cheesy goodness."

"Screw you. Give me one."

He snickered, handing me the slice he'd bitten into. He eyed me like he didn't think I'd take it. But my stomach wouldn't let me not. *And*, there was something intimate about sharing food. Biting where his teeth bit. Where his lips touched. Where his tongue—

I grabbed the slice and shoved it into my mouth, silencing my overactive, and apparently sex-deprived, inner voice.

"I figured you must've been to the point where you'd had it with hospital food."

"You did this for me?" I asked with a mouthful, savoring the cheesy goodness.

"Don't sound so surprised." He reached for another slice. "Hospital food sucks."

We both polished off a couple more slices in companionable silence. When neither of us could handle another bite, Drew picked up the box and carried it into the hallway. I envisioned him using his charm on the nurses at the nurses' station, probably leaving the remaining slices for them.

He returned pushing a wheelchair. "I've got something to show you."

* * *

The cool night air circled the hospital roof where Drew and I lay on the ground with our hands locked behind our heads. Neither of us had uttered a word as we stared at the overabundance of stars occupying the clear night sky.

It made no sense, but Drew's presence and laid-back demeanor soothed me. I could feel an intangible pull toward him. To be around him. To talk to him. To have his acceptance. To have his attention. Maybe I did need to consider the possibility that I'd never see him again.

"I saw your friend yesterday."

His words sucked the air right out of me. But I rebounded like the champ I was—or at least pretended to be. "Yes, she's single."

His head fell toward me. "That's not why I brought it up."

I didn't even bother looking at him. "Sure it is."

"It's not." Irritation colored his tone. "You don't get to tell me why I said something. You don't even know me."

My head fell to meet his gaze. "Oh, I know you all right."

I knew he wanted to stay annoyed at me, but his twitching lips said otherwise.

"Then why bring her up?"

His twitching morphed into a cocky grin. "Just wondering what you told her about me."

That grin. That adorable—maddening—grin. And just like that, my anger, jealousy—whatever it was going on with me—dissipated. "Oh, that's easy. I told her the truth. You're an annoying guy who won't leave me alone."

His unconvinced gaze told me I needed to work on my game. "Admit it. I'm wearing on you."

I purposely averted my eyes, turning my attention back to the sky. "Nope."

"Come on. I won't let it go to my head."

"Something's already gotten to your head because it's bigger than anyone's I've ever met before."

I could sense his grin widening. "Got that right."

Once my words and his response truly registered, heat crept into my cheeks.

Dammit.

"Admit it, Andi. I'm wearing on you. I promise I won't tell anyone."

I shrugged. "Fine. Maybe a tiny bit."

He laughed. "Usually doesn't take so long."

I didn't doubt that for a second.

My eyes latched onto an airplane moving across the sky like a shooting star. Too bad it wasn't. I would've wished to go back in time and not run on that road. Scratch that. I wouldn't have gone running at all. I shoved down the useless thought. "Any word on your tests?"

"No news is good news," he said, like he had it rehearsed.

"That's one way of looking at it." I racked my brain for something interesting to say. Something cute. Something witty. But I came up with nothing but more questions. "So what's going on with the draft?"

Drew released a deep sigh.

I worried I might've overstepped my bounds.

After a long pause, his voice broke the silence. "I declared my intent months ago. Now, if I withdraw, there are a lot of people it will affect. So I'm holding off until I'm positive of my decision."

I nodded, grasping the gravity of his situation. As an athlete, teams were banking on him. If he was slated as any early pick, endorsement deals were inevitably in the works. And no doubt millions of dollars were at stake. If he was hesitant about his desire to play professional football, he'd be hurting more than just himself. "Only you know what's right for you. It shouldn't matter what anyone else wants."

"You don't know my parents."

"What do they have to do with it?"

His attention moved back to the sky. "Everything."

I knew enough to let it go. He clearly had issues that a night on a rooftop with me wasn't going to fix.

"I can't remember the last time I just laid back and enjoyed the nothingness," he mused. "No decisions to make. No expectations. No motives in question."

"I know what you mean." And I did. I'd been so focused on my road to the Olympics, I'd rarely sat back to enjoy the journey. To enjoy much of anything, really. It's a wonder my ex put up with me as long as he did before cheating. My mind was always elsewhere.

"Thanks." Drew's voice travelled softly in the night air.

My head fell to the side while his eyes remained focused on the stars. "For what?"

"For being you."

I smiled. "Some might say it's a curse."

His head fell toward me. "Then they don't know you."

A moment passed between us. Our eyes didn't waver, if anything, the connection between us grew inexplicably stronger. An unspoken bond. A comradery. A friendship of sorts. Then his eyes dropped to my lips, zoning in on them for a long while.

The fact that my lips tingled at the mere thought of his lips on mine told me I was in big freaking trouble.

Then, as if I'd imagined it, he jumped to his feet, brushed tiny pebbles off the back of his jeans, and without a word delivered me back to my room.

Once I got settled onto my bed, I pulled my windblown hair up into a high ponytail. "Thanks for the change of scenery."

Drew shrugged like it was no big deal. "I'll stop by tomorrow." He turned to leave, then stopped and looked back over his shoulder. "Do you like games?"

My eyes narrowed. "What kind of games?"

His lips kicked up in the corners stretching to his eyes. "The fun kind."

Unsure what he was getting at, but normally up for anything, I shrugged. "Sure."

"Good. I'll be by tomorrow. Make sure you're wearing your big girl panties. You're gonna need them."

With that, he disappeared into the hallway, leaving me with a strong desire to see the sun rise so I could don those big girl panties.

CHAPTER FOUR

Drew walked into my room after dinner the following night with a brown paper bag in his hand. He closed the door behind him, eyeing me like a piece of meat.

Goose bumps scattered up my arms.

Since when did I like feeling like a piece of meat?

He approached the chair beside my bed and dropped down into it, keeping his eyes trained on mine.

"Hi?"

A devious smirk tipped his lips as he placed the bag on the floor and lowered my tray table in the space between us. He reached inside the crinkly bag, letting his hand linger. I'd give him props. He definitely knew how to pique my curiosity. His hand slid out grasping a shot glass. His eyes stayed on mine as he placed it on the empty tray table in front of him. Then he reached back in and pulled out a second glass.

"Thirsty?"

A slow sexy smile skated across his lips as he slid the glass in front of me. But he wasn't done. He reached back in the bag and pulled out a full bottle of vodka.

"Seriously?" I laughed.

He nodded. "You scared?"

"Scared I'm gonna drink you under the table."

He threw back his head and let loose a shoulder shaking laugh. So carefree. So comfortable. So unbelievably breathtaking.

But once it continued much longer than necessary, I crossed my arms over the UNC printed on my powder-blue T-shirt. "Are we playing a game or just trying to get sloppy drunk?"

His laughter subsided as he dug into his pocket and pulled out a quarter, holding it up so the fluorescent lights in my room reflected off it.

"So, we're wagering?"

He nodded. "And with the pain meds getting the liquor to your head quicker, you being drunk off your ass is just an added bonus."

I swallowed down. Hard.

"Now if I win..." He twisted his lips like he really needed to consider the stakes. "I get to give you a sponge bath."

He said it so matter-of-factly, it threw me for a loop. Though, it seemed like a win-win for me.

"If you win," he continued. "You give *me* a sponge bath."

"Who said I'd want to give you a sponge bath?" *I totally did.*

"Seriously? Have you seen me?"

I almost choked on the arrogance floating around the room. But in all honesty, I liked it. Too much. A guy who knew who he was and what he wanted turned me on. It's what I was drawn to. What I normally sought out. I nodded toward the vodka. "Where'd you get it?"

"My buddy Avery smuggled it in."

"All in an effort to get me drunk?"

His smile spread wide. "All in an effort to get you drunk *and* give you a sponge bath."

"Ever think of just asking?"

He stilled.

I let the notion linger for a long moment, then lifted my chin toward the quarter. "Bring it."

He unscrewed the bottle and filled both glasses to the brim. He clearly didn't plan on taking it easy on me. He nodded to my glass. "First one's for fun."

"So that's how it's gonna be?"

He lifted his shot to his lips and threw it back, completely unfazed by the liquor. "That's definitely how it's gonna be."

Ah, hell.

I lifted my shot, throwing it back like a true rock star. It burned a prickly path down my throat heating my body to the core. I wanted to shake my head and rid my taste buds of the disgusting liquid, but I'd perfected running with pulled muscles and sore ankles. No way a freaking drinking game would elicit weakness. Drew needed to believe I could do it. Believe I could do anything I set my mind to.

Or maybe it was me. Maybe I needed to believe that.

He handed me the quarter, brushing his fingertips against mine as he placed the coin into my palm.

Ignoring the tingling sensation resonating in my hand, I started the game, bouncing the coin off the surface of the tray table with incredible ease. It landed with a clink in his shot glass. I bit down on my bottom lip, resisting the urge to gloat.

Drew's eyes lifted from his glass to me. "Didn't realize I propositioned a ringer."

"Guess you don't know me as well as you think you do."

He stared me down as he dug the quarter out of his glass. Grasping the coin by the rim between his thumb and middle finger, like he'd perfected the fine art of Quarters a long time ago, his eyes shifted to the table. With finesse, he bounced the coin directly into my empty glass.

"Looks like we've both had some practice." I slid it from my glass, readying for my next shot. I lifted the coin, searching for the perfect spot on the table. As I was about to release it, Drew choked out an obnoxious cough. My coin bounced off the table, over the glass, and across the floor.

"Oops." He didn't even try faking remorse as he jumped to his feet.

"Oops my ass."

He stood over me with his lips twitching. "You think I did that on purpose?" Instead of grabbing the coin from its spot on the floor, he lifted the bottle and filled my glass to the brim.

"I think you're scared." I grabbed the shot, spilling some as I lifted it hastily to my lips. The alcohol singed my nose hairs. But I didn't let on. I tipped back my head and let the liquid flow down my throat. *Ughhh.*

Drew chuckled as he retrieved the quarter and dropped back into the chair. "I'll show you scared." He pushed himself to the edge of the seat, eyeing the glass like it required deep concentration to determine the distance between the quarter in his hand and the glass in front of me. Then he eyed it some more.

"Get on with it, would you?" I acted bored, but in all honesty, I needed to prolong the game. If not, I'd be drunk off my ass in no time. I stayed away from alcohol while training. So to say I was a lightweight would be an understatement.

Drew's eyes captured mine from across the table. "Good things come to those who wait."

Was it bad I wanted him to be talking about more than just getting the quarter in the glass?

His coin bounced off the table and sailed right into the glass in front of me. Again.

Dammit.

I dumped the coin into my hand like the thought of me being the only drunk one didn't faze me at all. I held the quarter for a second before bouncing it down on the table. It hit the rim of his glass and bounced off. Drew caught it before it hit the floor.

Fuuuck.

He didn't even hesitate. He just lifted the bottle and filled my glass to the top with a grin. "Drink up."

"Fuck off."

He threw back his head and howled. "She's feisty when she's drunk."

"She's not drunk. She's pissed." I threw back the shot. Thankfully, it stung a little less than the last.

"Can I just say, I like your feisty side. It's turning me on."

"I thought guys are genetically-predisposed to be turned on all day as it is?"

"All day. And *now* all night." That cocky smile slid across his face, the one I'd started to really like…or hate—I couldn't tell with my head's sudden fogginess. Not to mention, its sudden jump to things it had no business jumping to. Like the gray Henley tightly gripping his broad chest. His long fingers gripping the edge of the tray table. The zipper of his jeans—

"Ahem."

My eyes shot up. With the number of shots I'd ingested in a matter of minutes, with no end to our game in sight, I knew I was screwed. Why not embrace it. "Your turn."

His eyes never left mine as he picked up the quarter and aimed it at the table. It bounced and landed in the glass.

I threw up my hands. "You've got to be freaking kidding me."

He laughed as he settled back in the chair and crossed his sculpted arms.

Oh, yeah. He was hot.

"I hate you."

"But just think how nice my fingers are going to feel all over your skin."

Just the thought of his fingers anywhere near my skin sent shivers coursing through me. "A sponge bath implies a sponge will be used. No one said anything about fingers touching skin."

He nodded toward the coin in my glass.

I flipped him off which only made him laugh harder. "I'm serious. I hate you." I ignored the coin in my glass and for the hell of it—and because I *was* feeling a little feisty and didn't feel like missing again—I picked up the bottle and lifted it to my lips. I tipped back my head and took a nice long swig. When I lowered the bottle, Drew's clapping echoed off the empty walls.

"You're seriously my dream girl."

"Because I can drink you under the table?"

"Drinking me under the table would mean I've had more than one shot. And…" He leveled me with those pretty green eyes. "I've only had one shot."

I dumped the coin from my glass and held it out to him. He reached out, but instead of taking it, he held onto my hand, brushing his thumb lightly over my knuckles, leaving a numbness in its wake. And as much as I wanted to prolong it, to savor it, to see where it led, I needed to show strong. "Time to drink up, pretty boy."

"You think I'm pretty?"

I tilted my head, very aware that my hand remained in his strong grasp. "You know you are."

He stared at me long and hard, his eyes narrowing in contemplation. He wanted to say something. Something important. Something that could make the moment better if he only uttered the words. But just like that, the look disappeared, and his playfulness returned. "I just wanted to hear you admit it."

He released my hand and took the coin. This time the coin bounced to the side of the glass and into my lap. Part of me wondered if he'd missed intentionally.

Too many shots later, my eyes were mere slits. It was a miracle I could see anything.

"Do you give up?"

I tried to settle on one of the two Drews in front of me, before shaking my head. "I never give up." Oh, God. My words were ridiculously slurred.

He laughed. "Good to know. Because neither do I."

Even in my drunken stupor, I hoped his words referred to more than just our game. *What was wrong with me?* "Whose turn is it?"

"Asks the sober one?" he pointed out.

I stuck my tongue out at him. *Oh, yeah. I was totally sober.*

"Actually…" He stood up, stretching his arms over his head for no other reason than to give me a glimpse of the taut skin above his jeans as his shirt lifted. "I'm pretty beat."

Yummmm.

Shit. Did I say that out loud?

"I'm gonna head out," he said, dropping his arms to his sides.

My mouth parted. "What about my sponge bath?"

"You admit defeat?"

My eyes narrowed, trying to settle on a witty response. But since my drunken stupor rendered me incapable of a single coherent thought, a witty response was not happening.

"Tomorrow," Drew assured me. "I want you perfectly sober when I have my way with you."

Oh, sweet baby Jesus.

CHAPTER FIVE

I woke around noon sporting a head-pounding, stomach-churning hangover. Immediately, I rolled over and fell back to sleep. Luckily, the nurses and therapist left me alone. By dinner time, I felt good enough to keep down the saltine crackers that arrived with my broth.

"Someone have a rough night?"

My eyes slowly shifted to the door.

Drew, looking more than fine in his cargo shorts and black T-shirt, stood there with bouncing brows.

Bastard.

"I'm ready to collect."

"I still hate you."

He laughed as he entered my room. "You might change your mind once you hear what I have to offer." My eyes studied him curiously. Still hot. Still cocky. Still a pain in the ass. "I've decided I'd be willing to forgo the sponge bath."

"Oh?" A tinge of disappointment formed in the pit of my stomach.

"Why bother with a sponge bath when I can just jump right in the shower with you? I'm great with a loofah."

Though I'd never admit it, my body relaxed. "Great idea."

The smug smile slipped off his face. "Seriously?"

I leveled him with a look I hoped conveyed, "Get real."

"Yeah, I figured." He disappeared into the hallway.

Staring at the empty doorway, I wondered why I'd felt so let down by the notion of not getting a sponge bath. Had he already worked his way under my skin that much?

Within seconds, Drew returned with a bucket, washcloth, and towel and disappeared inside my bathroom.

As soon as the water sputtered, I let out a shaky breath. What was I doing? Was I really going to let this happen? Let some guy I barely knew put his hands all over my body?

My thoughts jumped to Logan. She had relationships—or at least relations—with strangers she took home from bars. By comparison, I'd known Drew far longer. And really? He wanted to give me a sponge bath. Big deal.

But the longer he remained in the bathroom, the harder my heart knocked against my chest. I tried focusing my breathing. Panting like a dog was so not cool. I was a grown woman for God's sake. It's not like I'd never been touched by a guy before.

Drew stepped out of the bathroom, moving toward me with such confidence. Such finesse. Such swagger. No way he learned it. People like him were born with it.

Bastard.

He placed the bucket full of sudsy water on my tray table, rolling it to the side of my bed. He kept his eyes on mine as he steeped the washcloth in the bucket and squeezed out the excess water.

Was he calling my bluff?

News flash. If anyone planned to back down, it'd be him.

"Close your eyes," he said with an irresistible rasp to his voice.

I did as told. His footsteps slowly retreated to the foot of the bed. I imagined him either staring down at me in my "booty shorts" and the white camisole Logan brought, evaluating my curves and bare skin. *Or* laughing at me for expecting an actual sponge bath.

I flinched when the warm cloth pressed to my right heel and moved slowly up the arch of my foot. A giggle burst out of me as I scrunched up my toes.

Drew yanked away the cloth. "Did you just giggle?"

My eyes snapped open, staring at his amused face at the foot of my bed. "I'm ticklish."

"Apparently. I've never had a girl giggle before."

"You've given a lot of sponge baths?"

He flashed a cocky grin. "Nope. You're definitely my first."

My belly quivered. Knowing I was his first anything did crazy things to my body.

I closed my eyes, accepting the fact that I was getting a sponge bath from a hot guy. And it *would* be relaxing. I willed myself with all I possessed not to giggle again like a little girl. I was twenty-two years old, God dammit.

Drew moved the cloth over the top of my foot. Thankfully, I wasn't ticklish there. He circled my ankle and dragged it back up to my toes, gently tugging on each one. Within seconds, the cloth disappeared from my skin.

Was that it? Was he done? Or was he contemplating his next move? With my cast covering most of my right leg, and my left knee still so sensitive, his options were limited.

Without warning, the cloth settled above my cast on top of my right thigh—almost searing my skin. Tiny tingles resonated not only there, but in all the sensitive spots above it. It would be nearly impossible to have his hand that close to my crotch without making a fool of myself.

I'd be the first to admit, it had been months since I'd had sex. But God. I was an embarrassment waiting to happen.

I steeled myself, focusing all my energy on breathing. Not the feeling of the cloth coasting over the top of my bare thigh. Not its journey down to my knee. Not the circular movement around my kneecap before moving to the side and gliding up to my hip in one slow stroke. Not the voyage back down to the side of my knee.

Without removing the cloth, Drew slipped it underneath, dampening the soft bend in my knee. From there, he slid it up the back of my thigh to the bottom of my shorts. I was no perv, but my mind instinctively jumped to indecent places. And knowing he'd yet to venture to my inner thigh, my traitorous heart pounded something fierce.

As if reading my thoughts, the cloth settled inches from the sensitive apex between my legs. I inhaled a sharp breath. Drew did the same. We were in dangerous territory and we both knew it.

I barely had time to focus on the too-intense-for-primetime-throbbing before he moved the cloth down to my inner knee. That's when it disappeared. The cloth. Not the sensation. That was there to stay, pulsing like the second hand on a clock.

A silence passed.

It took everything in me not to open my eyes. Where was he? What was he thinking? Was he having the same thoughts as me?

I heard a soft rustling then the cloth being submerged in the water. Within seconds, it ran up the arch of my left foot. This time I bit down on my bottom lip, stopping myself from even thinking of giggling.

Drew repeated the same path he'd taken on my right foot. But with no cast on my left calf, he trailed the cloth over my shin, skipping my knee and stopping on the top of my left thigh. There he grazed it down from my hip to my ankle, then underneath from my calf to the bottom of my shorts.

One would think I'd become accustomed to his touch, but the deep throbbing between my legs intensified, expanding out to my fingertips and toes.

The cloth settled on the inside of my left thigh. My breath hitched again. Drew had to have heard it.

Slowly—painfully slowly—he moved the cloth from the bottom of my shorts to the inside of my knee. At that point, my ball of nerves pulsed in tandem with my heartbeat.

He removed the cloth from my skin and dunked it back in the bucket. "So far so good?" he asked, his voice holding the deep rasp of someone just as turned on as me.

"Mmm-hmm." Couldn't he see my heaving chest?

The bed dipped as he sat beside me, the pressure of his muscular thigh resting up against my hip. With my eyes still closed, I could feel him shift toward me.

My body jolted when the damp cloth settled below my ear. I couldn't help imagining his lips in the same spot. Would they be tender caresses or open-mouthed bites? God, I wanted to find out. Now more than ever.

As the cloth skated down my neck, I wondered if he felt my quickened pulse protruding from my skin. If he did, he didn't let on as he slipped the skinny straps of my camisole off my shoulders.

With my eyes closed, my sense of sound became heightened. It's probably why I could hear Drew's shallow breathing as he followed the path over my collarbone and down to my shoulder.

Glad I'm not the only one affected.

He moved to my opposite ear, again dragging the cloth down my neck to my shoulder in one long sweep. Leaving my straps down, he trailed the cloth beneath my chin to the top of my cami. He stayed at my upper chest, gliding the cloth over my skin from left to right for a couple passes.

If only nothing existed between us. If only I knew what his actual touch felt like.

He lifted the cloth from my skin and pulled my straps back up.

I could hear the water splashing in the bucket as he steeped the cloth and twisted out the excess water. This time it landed on the top of my shoulder and glided down my arm in a slow torturous stroke to my fingertips. Goose bumps erupted all over my damp skin as the cool air attacked it, kick-starting major buzzing throughout my body.

He grasped my wrist and flipped over my arm, repeating the same path up the inside. When he moved over the sensitive bend in my arm, a giggle burst out of me.

"Again?" he laughed.

"Uh huh."

"You're so adorable."

I could feel myself grimace as he switched to my other arm. No one called Logan adorable. She was gorgeous. Beautiful. Hot. Those descriptions just weren't me. They'd never be me. I was too lanky. My hair hung poker-straight and never fell in pretty curls. And makeup rarely concealed the freckles dotting my nose. I needed to face the facts. While Drew held the power to make me forget what I'd lost—as well as the pain, anger, and bitterness that accompanied such a loss—he merely saw me as his buddy.

The realization tightened my chest and sobered the amazing feelings he'd been creating all over my body. My eyes popped open. "That felt amazing, but you can stop now."

Drew's eyes narrowed. "Are you kidding me? I don't half-ass anything. Especially when I've got a girl in bed. Now lay there and enjoy it." He dampened the cloth. "And keep your eyes closed."

Since I was in no position to get up and walk out of the room, I was truly at his mercy. It's why I begrudgingly closed my eyes.

No sooner had I, the cloth touched down on my forehead, drifting over it gently. I squeezed my eyes tighter, enjoying the unexpected warmth as it moved from my forehead, down to my right cheek, and over my nose. He removed the cloth and tugged gently on the bandage on my left cheek, slightly stinging the skin as he peeled it away.

I shuddered at the thought of the skin underneath. I'd been too afraid to look at it. Too afraid to discover I'd be left with a scar. A permanent reminder of my accident.

Drew didn't seem to mind what he saw, pressing the cloth to it for a long moment. "Relax. It's just a few scratches. It's almost healed."

I exhaled a deep breath, relieved his voice held no disgust.

Then, as if that hadn't relaxed me enough, he laid the cloth across my eyes and pressed gently into them. The pressure created a stillness throughout my body. My limbs hung limply. My mind became a blank slate.

Now I'd had massages before, especially after big races. But nothing—*nothing*—compared to the attention Drew paid to my body.

He lifted the cloth from my eyes and moved it to my lips. The pressure of his fingers drifting across my lips, the roughness of the cloth, and the warmth of the water prickled like the aftermath of a mind-blowing kiss.

"Mmmm," I murmured into the cloth, incapable of *not* uttering a sound.

Drew's sharp intake of breath was quickly followed by him yanking away the cloth. "Fuck it."

His large hands grabbed hold of my cheeks. My eyes flew open.

Before I could swallow down my surprise, his lips crashed down on mine, devouring me with fierce, determined movements. I tried to keep up—*God did I try*—but his lips moved with an unstoppable force. I opened my mouth slightly. That's all it took. His tongue plunged inside, playing a game of tag, lapping away, consuming me whole.

My hands lifted to his shoulders, slipping around his neck and tunneling into the thick hair at his nape. I pulled him closer, wanting to wrap my legs around him to ease the ache between my thighs. If I wasn't anchored to the bed, I would've. All. Night. Long.

Drew pulled back slowly, keeping his eyes locked on mine as his chest heaved as fiercely as my own. His tongue shot out and ran hungrily across his bottom lip.

"Didn't realize that was part of our wager," I whispered, as my numb lips fought to regain sensation.

Laughter erupted from him. "I know how to improvise."

"Yeah?" I couldn't stop my body from speaking for me. "I dare you."

Without hesitation, he leaned down, capturing my lips again for a long heart-pounding moment where I lost all sense of time. All sense of my situation. All sense of…everything. *God.* I could've gotten lost in him forever. His manly scent. His unrivaled control. His overwhelming being. He pulled away wearing his signature cocky grin, his eyes transfixed on my swollen lips. "Any time."

This time he sat up, causing my hands to slip away from his neck. Grabbing the bucket, he stood and walked into the bathroom, leaving me alone. Let me rephrase. Leaving me a complete pile of useless mush. I closed my eyes as my head fell deeper into my pillow.

What was that?

I'd like to say I took the time Drew remained in the bathroom pulling it together and calming my overly-excited body. But let's get real. He was hot and completely overwhelmed every part of my being with that kiss. Not to mention, surprised the hell out of me.

Drew stepped out of the bathroom and pulled open my door. Sounds from the hallway poured inside. A cruel reminder the outside world still existed. "I'll come by tomorrow," he said from his spot in the doorway.

I nodded, as he slipped out into the hallway and disappeared from my room like he'd never been there at all.

CHAPTER SIX

Doctor Evans massaged my right thigh, kneading it like dough to get the blood flowing down. "Feeling a little better?"

My legs, yes. The fact that Drew hadn't returned since the kiss the previous night—almost twenty-four hours before—not so much. "Both still throb a bit, but I figured that's to be expected."

"Especially with the physical therapist stretching your knee," he explained. "Glad to see she's got you out of the brace."

I nodded. "Me, too."

"Has she had you pedaling?"

"Yeah."

"Good." He gestured to my cast. "I'll be sending you down to our rehab facility to get you working on this leg once we get the cast off."

Out of the corner of my eye I noticed Drew slip inside my room. Was it bad that I could breathe normally again?

What had his kiss done to me?

What had *he* done to me?

I relied on one person for my happiness. And that was me. So why did it suddenly feel like Drew had control over it?

I peeked over at him standing in the corner of the room, his eyes focused on Doctor Evans' hands on my legs.

"The hardware inside will take some getting used to," Doctor Evans explained as his hands got dangerously close to my nether regions.

"Um, not sure I'm liking where this is going," Drew warned like a jealous boyfriend.

Though his jealousy made my insides all warm and fuzzy, I shot him a look over Doctor Evans' shoulder. "*Shush.*"

His eyes expanded. "Did you just shush me?"

"Yes."

He grinned. "What are you like five?"

Doctor Evans glanced over his shoulder at Drew.

"Must be," I shot back. "I've been hanging out with you, haven't I?"

Drew threw back his head and laughed. So childlike. So carefree. Not at all like a guy with his health a complete mystery and professional future so undecided. "Hanging out? I'd say we've been doing more than that."

My cheeks heated, and I found it difficult to meet Doctor Evans' eyes when he turned back to me. "How's your head?" he asked, completely ignoring Drew's comment.

Thank God.

"My headache's gone."

"That's good news." He removed his hands from my leg and stepped back. "Do you need anything before I head out? It's my anniversary and my wife made reservations."

"I'll be fine." I glanced to Drew. "I'm in good hands."

Doctor Evans glanced to Drew before nodding. "I'll stop by to check on you tomorrow."

"Okay. Happy Anniversary."

"Thanks." He smiled as he headed to the door and disappeared into the hallway.

Drew pushed off the wall and stalked toward me. "Was it as good for you as it was for him?"

"You just heard him. He's married."

"He's married. Not blind."

I tilted my head. "Is this you being funny?"

The mattress dipped as he sat beside me, kicking up his feet and letting his jean clad legs lay parallel to my cast. He leaned back beside me, sharing my pillow. His fresh powder scent invaded my senses, throwing a damn party in every little crevice. "No, I wasn't being funny. But girls definitely love the sense of humor."

My head fell toward him. His did the same. Inches separated us as I stared into his eyes, examining the flecks of mint green and the darker ring circling his iris. "Is that the only thing they love?"

His eyes dropped to my lips. "Well, the abs seem to be a crowd pleaser. And the eyelashes." His eyes lifted to mine. "What is it with girls and long eyelashes?"

I moved my head from side to side. "No idea." I inched closer, giving him the subtle go-ahead. "We like hats pulled down low, too."

"Is that right?" He pressed his lips to mine, caressing them with soft, gentle kisses for a long body-numbing moment. When he pulled back, I didn't make it easy, tugging his bottom lip with my teeth before letting it pop free. He smiled against my lips. "I've gotta go grab dinner with my parents. They're stopping by."

My head snapped back. "Will you be okay?"

He nodded. "Been handling them for twenty-two years. What's an hour? You gonna be around later?"

I shook my head. "I've got a hot date. He's taking me out clubbing. So..." I shrugged.

He reeled back enough to peruse my face. "Clubbing?"

"Oh yeah. I'm thinking about wearing a short dress to show off my cast. And if I'm feeling daring, I might even throw on my hooker heels."

His eyes narrowed. "Hooker heels?"

I nodded, keeping my eyes trained on his. "Easily six inches."

He lowered his voice to a sexy rasp. "I'd like to see you in those some time."

Goosebumps popped up all over my body as he rolled off the bed, leaving my breathing labored and my heart galloping like a damn race horse.

As if he sensed it, he turned back with a lopsided smirk and pressed his hands into the mattress. He leaned down, his face lingering over mine, his proximity both tempting and torture. "I'm thinking summer around here might not be so bad after all."

"Oh, yeah? Why's that?"

He inched closer. But instead of indulging me with an answer, he pressed his lips to my forehead. "See you after your hot date."

I pushed out an exasperated breath as he stood and walked toward the door.

He stopped in the doorway, turning to face me one last time. "Just promise me one thing."

"Don't play quarters with anyone while you're gone?" Sometimes I just couldn't resist being a smart-ass.

He shook his head, his face suddenly serious. "Don't go forgetting about me."

"That'd be pretty hard to do."

His head tilted to the side, his eyes pensive. "Why's that?"

I shrugged. If he wasn't going to give an inch, neither was I.

Drew's slow spreading grin was the last thing I saw before he disappeared into the hallway. And only then, only when he was down the hall and out of air shot, did I exhale the breath I'd been unknowingly holding.

* * *

"Hi, Andi." A woman I'd never met before stepped into my room. "I'm Doctor Fallon." She wasn't wearing a white coat like the other doctors, instead a pinstripe blue pant suit with her name badge dangling from her pocket. She looked at the empty chair beside my bed. "Mind if I sit?"

I shook my head. It wasn't like Drew had returned from dinner yet.

She sat down and flipped open a manila file folder, scanning its contents. "How have you been feeling since your accident?"

"I'm sorry. But what kind of doctor are you?"

She glanced up, her face composed. "A psychiatrist."

My eyes stretched wide. "Do I need a psychiatrist?"

"Not exactly. But sometimes patients with cerebral edema display adverse reactions."

"Adverse reactions? What does that mean?"

She uncrossed her legs and folded her hands over the file folder on her lap. "Well, some complain of severe headaches. Some report memory lapses. Some experience hallucinations."

My brows pinched. "Where do I fit into all that?"

"Well, Doctor Evans mentioned—"

My eyes flared as my voice rose. "Mentioned what?" I struggled to pull enough air into my lungs as I sensed my life about ready to be turned on its head. Again.

Doctor Fallon leaned forward. "There's no reason to become alarmed. He simply mentioned you'd made some comments when the two of you were alone earlier."

"Alone? We weren't alone. Drew was here."

She cocked her head. "Drew?"

"Yes. Drew."

"Okay." She said it like she didn't believe me.

Why didn't she believe me?

"Some of the nurses also mentioned they've witnessed you carrying on conversations while you've been alone."

My chest constricted as my mind reeled at warp speed. Sure my internal ramblings had been working overtime recently, but I never talked to myself. That was just insane.

We sat for a long time, neither saying a word. I gathered it was her approach. Give the patient time to think. Time to realize they were crazy. Well, I wasn't falling for it.

After what felt like an eternity of silence, Doctor Fallon stood from the chair and walked out of my room. I wanted to yell after her, "And stay out!" But that wouldn't have proven my sanity. At. All.

I closed my eyes and raked my fingers through my hair. Talking to myself? Who did she think she was? Who did Doctor Evans and the nurses think they were? If I was talking to myself—which I wasn't—I had every reason to. I'd been stripped of my dream. Of my ability to walk. Of my independence. Cut a girl some freaking slack.

Doctor Fallon walked back in pushing a wheelchair. "I'd like you to take a walk with me."

"Where?"

"To see Drew."

"He's having dinner with his parents."

She eyed me across the room. I could see in the slight tightening around her eyes that she didn't believe me. But why? "We can always just wait for him to return then, can't we?"

Doctor Fallon wheeled me down to the fourth floor. We made our way through the long hallway, halting when a hefty nurse with fire engine red hair and an angry glare stepped in front of my chair.

"Excuse us, Margie," Doctor Fallon said.

Margie dug her hands into her wide hips, her stare locked on Doctor Fallon's. "I'm going to say this again. I don't think it's a good idea for her to be down here."

"And I'll repeat what I said," Doctor Fallon said calmly. "It is."

I looked to Margie. "If it's his parents you're worried about, he already told me they're tough. But I'm pretty sure I can handle them."

Margie's eyes narrowed as they jumped between Doctor Fallon and me.

"See?" Doctor Fallon said way too cheerfully to be authentic. "She's a strong young lady. She can handle it." With that, she moved me around Margie and continued down the hallway, stopping outside the last room on the right. The door sat slightly ajar, but not enough to see inside. She didn't bother knocking. Instead, she just pushed it open.

Once I could see inside the dimly lit room, my heart stopped beating. I sat paralyzed. Stunned. Scared. Confused. Margie's concern became painfully clear. And it wasn't Drew's parents.

My trembling hands grabbed hold of my wheel grips, and I slowly rolled inside.

My eyes drifted over the sight before me. Drew lay in bed with his eyes closed. A rubber mask covered his nose and mouth. His chest rose and fell as a ventilator pushed air into his lungs.

I stopped beside his bed and grasped his limp hand. No matter how hard I tried, I would've never been able to warm his icy flesh. With my eyes locked on him, and my heart now beating out of my chest, I asked the only question that mattered. "What happened?"

Doctor Fallon placed her hand on my shoulder. "He was in a serious accident."

"An accident? I was just with him."

Her grip on my shoulder tightened. "Andi. Drew's been in a coma for almost a week."

CHAPTER SEVEN

Waves of agony rolled through my body as I sat at Drew's bedside. I'd carried on an imaginary relationship with a guy in a catatonic state. There was no mistaking it. I was bat shit crazy.

How had I allowed it to happen?

How had I given up control of my mind?

Of my sanity?

Doctor Fallon wanted me to talk about my feelings. Talk about how it felt to discover I'd constructed the entire "relationship" in my head. But I respected her for not pushing the issue when I sat silently stunned. And though she began me on medication to relieve my swelling *and* made me promise to meet with her the following day, I appreciated her allowing me to stay with Drew even after she left.

I stared at his idle body. At the tubes and machines keeping him breathing. At the dim hospital room he'd been in for almost a week. None of it made any sense. I'd never seen Drew before that day in my room. Never even heard of him. How could I have known his name? How could I have known what he looked like? How could it have all been in my head?

I watched Drew's chest lift and drop as his cold limp hand remained in my grasp like a dead weight. Just the day before, the same hand had given me an amazing sponge bath. Scratch that. The day before he'd been in a *coma*.

How would I ever be able to wrap my head around that?

Somehow, even with everything so screwed up, so unbelievable, so far from normal, being close to Drew comforted me. Like we were in it together.

Together?

God, I was so pathetic. We didn't even *know* each other.

The longer I sat there, the more my mind fell devoid of all rational thoughts. All I could focus on was my waning sanity. My inability to differentiate between truth and fiction. My sad pathetic life.

As more time lapsed, the clicking and whistling of the ventilator became a messed up lullaby. And by some strange miracle, my exhausted and confused body drifted off into a much needed slumber.

* * *

"What...the...fuck?"

My head shot up from the side of Drew's bed. Given the drool on my cheek and the orange glow outside the window, I'd been asleep for quite some time. My eyes flew to Drew. A loud whooshing came from the mask hanging off his mouth. His eyes were barely open but they stared directly at me. "You're awake," my voice squeaked in surprise.

He continued staring, but didn't speak.

"Let me get the doctor."

His hand, still in my grasp, twitched. Was he trying to say something? Trying to stop me?

"I'll be right back," I assured him, slipping my hand free and reversing my chair out of his room. I'd like to say I did it with grace, but I bumped everything and its mother before making it into the hallway.

Margie and a younger nurse stepped out of the room next door.

"Drew's awake! He's awake."

They didn't hesitate, rushing by me right into his room.

My stomach twisted as I watched helplessly from the doorway as they checked his vitals while firing off questions.

"Can you tell me your name, honey?" Margie asked him, wrapping a blood pressure cuff around his arm.

"How about your birthday?" The other nurse asked, swiping a thermometer across his forehead.

"Do you remember being brought in?" Margie asked, her eyes focused on his blood pressure and heart rate readings flashing on the machine beside his bed.

Drew's eyes followed them and their rapid movements, but he didn't answer.

"Your parents have been here to visit. Do you have any recollection of that?" Margie asked.

Silence greeted her yet again.

Tears filled my eyes as I watched the heartbreaking scene play out…for so many reasons.

Margie's eyes shifted to me in the doorway. She hurried over. "Honey, you're going to have to go back to your room."

"Is he going to be okay?"

Her lips twisted. "He's awake. That's a good start."

* * *

I didn't sleep after leaving Drew's room. Instead, I researched comas and the likelihood of recovery on my phone. Most websites claimed patients required three days to recover for every day they were unconscious—if, of course, they'd shown positive signs like eye movement and attempted speech. Some sites gave little hope for recovery, all but guaranteeing a vegetative state.

But Drew *had* spoken. He'd heard me. He'd heard the nurses. That had to mean something.

While in research mode, I looked into the side effects of cerebral edema. Something I probably should've done a lot sooner. Ironically, confusion topped the list. Would've been nice to know that *before* learning I was nuts.

After a quick breakfast, I hurried downstairs. I knew Doctor Fallon wanted to talk, but I needed to see Drew with my own two eyes before I could talk about my feelings. With my reality clearly distorted, I needed to be sure what occurred the previous night had indeed occurred.

With my heart practically bursting out of my chest, I neared his room. Down deep I knew he wouldn't know me. Wouldn't remember how he helped me. Wouldn't remember our brief time together. But a small part of me held out hope that he would. That there'd be at least an inkling of recognition. Something. Anything.

Voices inside Drew's room stopped me short of his door. I rolled the last couple feet, just enough to spy a well-dressed woman in the chair beside him. A tall man, with broad shoulders and dark hair similar to Drew's, paced the floor.

I backed up, keeping Drew in my line of vision while remaining hidden from his visitors.

"What the hell were you thinking?" the man growled.

Drew didn't speak, though his eyes trailed the man.

"Drew." The woman leaned forward, grasping Drew's hand. "Your father and I have been beside ourselves with worry."

"Look at him," the man balked, throwing his hand out in Drew's direction. "He doesn't even give a damn."

"We need you to tell us the truth," the woman implored. "We need you to give us a little something here."

Drew closed his eyes, turning his head away from them.

Was he unable to speak? Was he ignoring them?

His silence didn't deter them. They waited him out, shooting each other angry glares across the room. I couldn't tell who they despised more. Each other or Drew. But I had to hand it to him. He kept his eyes closed.

"He knew exactly what he was doing," the man said loud enough for Drew to hear.

"We don't know that."

"The hell we don't. He's always been calculated." He turned to Drew. "Do you hear me you selfish son of a bitch?"

Drew didn't move.

"You ruined everything! *You* did this." He grabbed the tray table and slammed it into the nearest wall, sending its contents clattering all over the floor.

Drew's eyes snapped open.

The woman jumped to her feet, throwing her skinny body in between them. "Bruce!" She braced her hands on his chest as he pressed toward Drew.

It couldn't be stopped. I flew into the room. "Stop it!"

The man and woman froze. Their heads whipped toward me.

"Are you insane?" I couldn't hide the mix of shock and disgust in my voice. "He just came out of a coma."

The man dropped his head and shook it slowly from side to side. "He's even got the cripples fooled."

"Fuck you," I spat across the room.

His empty eyes lifted, latching coldly onto mine. "Oh, and a classy one to boot."

Hate deeper than I ever thought possible churned inside me. "First of all, you don't know me."

"Thankfully," he murmured.

"Second." I bit back the choice words itching to fly out. "He hasn't even been awake for twelve hours and look at the way you're treating him. You should be ashamed of yourself."

A scary smile split his lips. "Oh, sweetheart, he's got you so deluded it's not even funny." His amused tone turned condescending. "But you're wasting your time. There's no money. There's no garage full of cars. There's no yacht. He's a has-been." A spray of spit followed his harsh words as he glared at Drew. "A never-was."

The woman grabbed him by the arm and pulled him out of the room and down the hallway.

I looked back to Drew who stared at the empty doorway, his eyes vacant.

I should've gone back upstairs. I should've carried on as though I'd never "met" him or his whacked-out parents. I should've done what my gut told me to do. But my curiosity and desire to be sane kept me there.

Nowhere near stealthy rocking the wheelchair, I rolled toward his bed, this time bumping into the tray table his lunatic father had thrown across the room. The loud noise caused Drew's narrowed eyes to shoot to mine.

"I think they're gone," I offered.

He blinked, as if trying to refocus his eyes.

I stopped my chair at his side. "I would've thought they'd be happy you're awake."

He stared at me with those pretty eyes encased by thick long lashes. They were exactly the same, right down to the lighter flecks etched in them. But they were missing the indelible twinkle and reverence he normally showed me. Maybe it was the effect of the coma. Maybe it was his parents' behavior and abrupt departure. Maybe it was the fact that he had no clue who I was.

"Well, on the bright side, at least they came. Mine are out of the country. They haven't even been here." It felt strange confiding in someone who already knew my story—at least in my head he did. "My best friend stops by, but she's usually in a rush to get back to campus. Back to the land of the living."

I glanced at the machines surrounding him. The ones that, up until last night, kept him alive. A blanket covered his body, but I could still see the tubes and wires running underneath. I wondered how long it would take for him to return to normal.

Normal.

Like I even knew what normal was. For him *or* me.

"Guess you had a pretty bad accident."

He closed his eyes and turned his head away from me, just like he'd done with his parents.

I considered waiting him out. I knew I could do it. I was stubborn like that. But as more time passed and he still hadn't moved or looked my way, I assumed he'd drifted off to sleep.

I certainly didn't want to be around for round two with his parents, so just as discouraged as I'd been the previous night, I reversed my chair out of his room—carefully this time—and headed upstairs for my inevitable appointment with Doctor Fallon.

CHAPTER EIGHT

"I just feel so ridiculous."

Doctor Fallon stared across the three feet of space separating us in her office. "Even though you know the edema caused it?"

I nodded. "I still can't understand how I could've known so many things about him."

"You were in and out of consciousness after surgery," Doctor Fallon explained. "It's possible you overheard nurses talking. Drew's presence has caused quite some excitement around here, especially amongst the nursing staff."

My shoulders dropped on a sigh. "Maybe."

"Let me ask you something." She uncrossed her pant-clad legs and folded her hands in her lap. It was definitely her go-to technique to put patients at ease.

Newsflash. I was nowhere near at ease.

"Was there anything positive that came out of the experience?"

I scoffed. "The experience? That's what we're calling it?"

"You're going to have to stop beating yourself up over this, Andi. You're not crazy. Do you hear me? These things happen to normal people."

"Sure they do," I mumbled.

"Listen. It's my job to help work you through this."

"Work me through it?" At that point my incredulous voice rose. "I had a freaking relationship with a guy in a coma. There is no working that out. In my head—in my memory—it very much happened. It was as clear as day. I can recite conversations and things we did. I cannot allow you to convince me it didn't happen."

"Why not?"

"Because then I know without a doubt that I'm crazy. And I won't let myself believe that."

"Then let me say it again. You are *not* crazy."

I rolled my eyes.

"Can I ask you something?"

I shrugged.

"Do you think elderly people who suffer from Alzheimer's are crazy?"

I crossed my arms across my chest. "Of course not. They can't help what happens to them."

"Exactly. Nor could you. You suffered severe swelling. If the doctors knew you'd been having hallucinations, you would've been given medication immediately. But no one knew."

My head withdrew. "*I* didn't know."

"The medication will help with that. I assure you."

"And what if it doesn't? What if I really am crazy?"

Doctor Fallon let out a long, frustrated breath. "Why don't we get back to my initial question. Is there anything positive that came from the experience?"

I stared across the room at the framed diplomas hanging over her desk. She didn't need the paperwork to validate it. Just speaking to her for a brief time it was obvious she was a smart woman. She was someone who knew exactly what she wanted. She went after it. And here she sat doing it.

I wished I could've been that sure of myself. I had absolutely no idea what I wanted anymore. I had no idea who I even was. How did she ever expect me to know how to answer her question?

"Andi?"

I glanced back to her. "He made me forget."

A small smile tugged at her lips.

"He made me look forward to the next day. He made me ignore what happened to me. And for a little while, I wasn't alone in all this."

Doctor Fallon nodded. "Good answer."

Tears glossed my vision. It was all too much. The realization of what I'd just admitted—to her and myself. The reality of losing my main distraction. The sadness of being primarily alone again.

* * *

"Holy shit!" Logan reached across the table and snatched a handful of potato chips from my plate. "I've never met a real life whack-job before."

I watched the doctors and nurses in colorful scrubs hurrying through the cafeteria lines grabbing quick lunches. Life for them progressed as usual. For me, my sanity remained in question with each passing breath.

"So, explain to me how this happened," Logan said with a mouthful. "What'd the shrink say?"

"She said it's common for cerebral edema patients to become confused and potentially hallucinate."

"You did more than hallucinate. You got to second base with the guy."

I closed my eyes, trying not to let her words send me into a tailspin. If I pretended it never happened, I was fine. But once I thought about it—or talked about it—I felt out of control of my own thoughts. Feelings. Well-being.

Logan flashed a grin. "Look at it this way. At least you hallucinated a hot guy who actually exists."

I exhaled an unassured breath. "None of it makes any sense."

"Says the nut."

I didn't even bother flipping her off. It was difficult to get angry at her when everything in my life was so screwed up. My head. My heart. My future. "It felt so real." I closed my eyes, burying my face in my palms.

"I know." I could hear the sincerity in her voice. Her joking, no matter how inappropriate at times, was just a cover when she didn't know what else to say. And I loved her for it.

"I really wanted it to be real," I said, muffled by hands.

"Why can't it be?"

I let my hands drop to my lap as I stared across the table at her. "Because he doesn't know me."

"He didn't know you a week ago either, and look how far you got."

As much as I wanted to believe she had a point, believe there was hope, everything in me told me the whole situation was messed up beyond repair.

* * *

"Your swelling's begun to decrease," Doctor Fallon informed me during our second session.

"How soon before I can stop the meds?"

She shook her head at my eagerness. "Don't be in such a rush. Your long term health is our top priority here."

My eyes flashed away, feeling ready to jump out of my own skin. I hated taking meds. And I hated feeling crazy.

"In the short term," she continued. "I have an idea. More of an experiment really."

My eyes flashed back to her. "Should I expect cheese with my lab rat status?"

She cocked her head, eyeing me seriously. "Work with me here, Andi. I think since you're not a fan of medicine, there might be something else that could help."

The following day, I rolled up outside Drew's room. Doctor Fallon thought, in addition to the meds, it would be healthy for me to face my hallucination head on. She also thought it would be good for Drew to have someone talking to him. I wasn't as sure as she was of her little experiment, but I showed up nonetheless.

I could see him alone inside, watching television on his bed looking more like the Drew I knew in a red T-shirt and cargo shorts. I dragged in a deep breath and lifted my knuckles, tapping lightly on the door.

His eyes flashed to me.

My lips tipped to one side, trying to feign normalcy, all the while my heart knocked behind my ribcage like a trapped bird. "In the mood for a visitor?"

His eyes shot back to the television.

O-kay.

I glanced around his empty room. If he was the hot shot football star my Drew claimed to be—the one Logan said had thousands of followers—weren't people concerned? Where were the gifts and well wishes? Where was the revolving door of visitors?

I rolled inside, parking myself beside his bed. His eyes remained on the television, giving me time to strategize. Time to figure out what the hell I was doing.

"Did the nurses toss your flowers and balloons?" I asked.

His eyes didn't move from the television.

"I never understood the concept of bringing gifts to a hospital. If someone's sick, the last thing they want are some smelly flowers or annoying balloons floating all over the place. Am I right?"

Still nothing.

Doctor Fallon warned me it wouldn't be easy, claiming many coma survivors were unable to form coherent sentences for some time. As a result, some displayed agitation, aggression, even amnesia after waking. So against my better judgment, I kept at it. "I guess it makes people feel better. Makes them feel like they're doing something to help you deal."

I glanced to the television. *SportsCenter* played on the screen. My eyes shot away. Any mention of the Olympics would crush me, so I averted my eyes. "After my accident, my roommate helped me deal." I shook my head, hating that he had no idea I was talking about him. "The hospital actually put me in with a guy when I first got here. They moved him once I recovered from surgery, though."

For some reason, I expected that small bit of information to affect him. To cause him to glance my way, twitch, move. Something. But being there obviously wasn't working...for either of us. He needed a doctor to get him talking, and I needed to go on with my life not knowing this Drew.

My eyes drifted to the window. To the bright blue sky outside. I thought back to the races I'd lost—and there had been plenty throughout my career—but I'd never given up. I fought. I always fought. And in that moment, I didn't need to fight for Drew. I needed to fight for me. My stability depended on it.

I looked back to him. "I guess it's against hospital policy to have a guy and girl in the same room. He said they were concerned we'd go at it like rabbits." I smiled at the recollection. "He was the one who got me moving. He didn't let me sulk or stay in my room. He pushed me to get better."

I huffed out a long frustrated breath, wishing his silence wasn't pissing me off so much. Because, honestly, speaking to someone who could hear me but wouldn't acknowledge me was absolute torture. Especially when desperately needed to feel sane again.

But he'd just woken from a coma. It wasn't fair for my expectations to be so high. The voice I'd heard the night he woke up—the words that shook me from sleep—must've been my own overactive imagination.

Wouldn't have been the first time.

I stared down at my cast. "At least you don't have screws in your leg. I'll probably be setting off alarms from here on out." I wasn't even talking to him anymore. Just vocalizing what I'd been too afraid to admit to myself. "And forget running. That part of my life's over."

Drew finally turned his head, staring at me like I'd spoken a foreign language.

I shrugged. "But just like you, I'll survive."

His eyes narrowed. Was he angry? Confused?

"I broke my leg and tore my ACL. But that's not even the best part." I tapped the side of my head. "I've got some swelling up here that makes me hallucinate."

He continued staring.

"The doctor said it's a side effect." Why was I telling him this? And why couldn't I shut up? "My best friend Logan would say I've been a little screwy for years. You know how sympathetic friends can be." Yup. Still rambling.

And Drew was still staring. "What do you want?"

My eyes expanded at the sound of his weak voice. "You can talk?" *And the award for the most obvious goes to…* "I mean, no one knew if you'd…" I searched for the right word.

"Live?"

I nodded, uncomfortable with the harsh reality of it all.

"Lucky me."

I flinched at the cold clip to his voice. "You didn't want to *live*?"

He stared back at me for a long time, his eyes searing into mine like I should've known the answer. Like I should've known the truth behind his silence. But why would I? I didn't know him.

The longer I sat in his presence and held his gaze, the more I could see he was different. Different from the guy who befriended me. Got me drunk. Gave me a sponge bath. Kissed me.

Gahhhh.

When was it going to sink in that he'd never done any of those things?

"You a reporter?" he asked gruffly.

I closed my eyes and my shoulders dropped. I'd hoped against all odds that he'd somehow know me. Somehow remember our brief time together. Somehow remember he was the one person who took my mind off everything I'd lost. Now it was clear he didn't have the same recollections as me. "No. I'm not a reporter."

"A groupie?" His voice was harsh and cut like a knife. "Because if you're offering—" He reached down and unbuttoned his shorts. "It's been a while."

My eyes widened as I drew a sharp breath. Reality clobbered me over the head as I grasped my wheels and reversed my chair. In my sudden haste, I rolled forward, slamming into Drew's bed and jostling his entire body and mine in the process.

"Fuck," he grumbled.

He had that right.

I somehow managed to get my wheels to spin me around and then hauled ass away from this Drew as quickly as possible.

I texted Logan on the way back to my room, filling her in on the awkward encounter. If anyone could make light of the situation, it was her. No sooner had I settled back onto my bed, my phone rang.

Before I even said hello, she roared with laughter. "He thought you were there for *that*?"

"Yup."

"Well, I guess the blonde hair and hot little bod must've given him the wrong impression."

"Um…thanks?"

"Are you gonna tell the shrink?"

"Tell her what? He's horny?" I didn't think she could laugh any harder, but she did. "Still here. Still waiting for my best friend to make me feel better."

Her laughter subsided. "So, getting back to where you left off might not be as easy as I thought."

I watched the nurses bustling by my open door. "No kidding."

"Buck up, girl. You're down, not out. I want you to march down there—"

"I can't walk."

"You know what I mean. Go down there and show him you're no one's hooker. Because the Andi Parker I know and love would never let some guy proposition her like that without taking her heel to his balls."

I scoffed. "That's not exactly what he was looking for when he unzipped."

"Good point. But believe me when I say, I may not be some overpaid shrink, but I'm not completely convinced your guy isn't in there somewhere."

I appreciated her encouragement. But she was wrong.

My Drew was gone.

* * *

I felt myself nodding off after working with the visiting physical therapist. My knee felt a little stronger, but the workout itself wiped me out. It was crazy how easily I could run for miles not even a month before. Now I could barely even endure a brief therapy session.

"Andi?" a deep voice whispered.

My eyes snapped open.

An older man in a wrinkled plaid button-down and jeans slipped into my room, closing the door quietly behind him. He walked toward me, stopping at the chair beside my bed and grasping onto the back with both hands. Something seemed off about the guy. Probably his twitchy eyes jumping around the room before settling hungrily on me.

"Can I help you?" I felt myself inching away from him.

He flashed a smile, answering way too eagerly. "Absolutely."

I discreetly gripped the remote control at my hip, finding the call button with my thumb, seconds away from pressing it.

"I'm Jim Forester, a sports reporter with the *Times*. I was hoping to ask you some questions for a story I'm working on."

"A story? About what?"

He slipped his phone out of his pocket and tapped the screen, holding it out to record our conversation. "Your accident, of course."

"My accident? I didn't realize it was news."

"Are you kidding? Promising athlete ends up—" The door flung open, cutting off his words.

The head nurse on my floor walked in. The second her eyes landed on the reporter, they flared. "I told you people not to come back here." Her words were cold and accusatory.

He stuffed his phone into his pocket. "No harm, no foul. Ms. Parker and I were just chatting. Isn't that right, Ms. Parker?"

My eyes jumped from Jim to the nurse, but her eyes remained locked on him. "I'll tell you what I told the rest of them," she said, her flushed cheeks mirroring her maroon scrubs. "Stay out of this building or the authorities will be called. And mark my words. You will be charged with trespassing."

His eyes fell to mine. "Looks like we're going to have to finish our chat some other time." He turned on his heels and walked out of my room.

I looked to the nurse, expecting an explanation, but she, too, turned to leave. "There have been others?"

She stopped in her tracks, slowly turning and nodding.

"Do you know why he wants to do a story on me? Why my injury's news?"

Her eyes jumped away, avoiding me like a bad car accident.

"Please tell me what's going on."

Her shoulders tensed. "Doctor Fallon gave strict orders. You're not to be bothered by anyone."

My face fell. "Why?"

"She doesn't want anyone getting in the way of your progress."

"My progress?" my voice squeaked. "Does she still think I'm unhinged? What aren't you telling me?"

The nurse laughed uncomfortably. "She's just being cautious. You know, better safe than sorry." She tugged lightly on my blankets. "Why don't you get some rest. And next time a reporter sneaks in here, do us all a favor and press the call button."

* * *

I spent the next few days surrounded by the same four walls bored out of my mind. Logan had been busy gearing up for finals and planning some end-of-year sorority soiree, so besides the occasional visit from the PT to stretch out my knee and appointments with Doctor Fallon, I'd been alone. It's probably the reason I sat in my wheelchair outside the fourth floor elevator. Not because Doctor Fallon encouraged me to continue my visits with Drew, but because I wanted a friend in this place. I wanted someone to laugh with. To commiserate with.

Did it really matter this Drew wasn't my Drew? Did it really matter he didn't know me? Did it really matter he thought I was a hooker? *Okay. Scratch that one.* We were two people stuck in a hospital. Two people unhappy with our circumstances. Two people with more in common than most.

I inhaled a deep breath and rolled down the hallway.

Margie spotted me and hurried around the nurse's station. "Hi, honey."

I offered a smile, motioning with my head toward Drew's room. "How's he doing?"

"You've been in there. You tell me."

"I haven't been by in days."

"Why's that?"

I shrugged.

"You'd tell me if he's spoken to you, wouldn't you?"

I swallowed around the guilty knot that suddenly formed in my throat. "Why would he speak to me? I thought he couldn't speak?"

I watched her shoulders sag. Was she disappointed? Relieved? "Well, I'm relying on you to come get me as soon as he decides to. Okay?"

Not wanting to perjure myself any more than I already had, I kept my lips sealed and nodded.

"Just so you know," Margie continued. "Doctor Fallon filled me in on what happened with you."

"My accident?"

She shook her head. "Your edema."

I scoffed. "So much for patient confidentiality."

She smiled in a grandmotherly way. "Well, if it makes you feel better, I'm the one who asked."

My brows slanted in.

"You mentioned that Drew told you about his parents." She tilted her head. "I knew that wasn't possible."

"So, you think I'm crazy?"

She shook her head. "On the contrary. I think you're one of the lucky ones."

"Lucky ones?"

"Well, when you work in a hospital as long as I have, you see things. Things you can't always explain. Things that make you do a double take, question your sanity." She laughed. "I know Doctor Fallon attributes your experience to the edema, but I've had enough of my own experiences to know that sometimes things happen and they just don't make any sense. At least the type of sense that sits well with society."

I lowered my voice, fearing someone would overhear our bizarre conversation. "What kind of experiences?"

"Any nurse who's worked in a hospital or been around the terminally ill will tell you that a person's soul is a powerful thing."

I cocked my head. Soul? Was she for real?

"I'm telling you. When a soul's leaving a body, it has all sorts of fun with the living."

My eyes flashed around. Was anyone else hearing this?

"I've see objects move," she continued. "Heard voices calling out to me when I was alone. Witnessed televisions popping on and off. Felt tugs on my clothes and gusts of cool air passing by me in storage closets and windowless rooms."

My eyes narrowed as I attempted to grasp her words. "I don't understand. You think Drew died?"

She shook her head. "No. Mr. Slater is very much alive. But who's to say if while he was unconscious, he didn't contemplate leaving. That's when the souls get even more creative."

I crossed my arms, waiting for her to burst into laughter. Or cameras from a hidden video show to reveal themselves. "Come on. You can't really believe that?"

Margie shrugged, her face void of amusement. "You asked what I experienced. Those are some of the things. So, to answer your question, yes. I really do believe. The better question is, do you?" She didn't wait for my answer. She turned and walked down the hall, disappearing into one of the rooms.

I sat in that spot for a long time replaying her outrageous words in my head. Which explanation made more sense? Her theory of souls and otherworldly occurrences? Or Doctor Fallon's clinical diagnosis?

I wasn't one of those people who dismissed the ideas of ghosts and spirits. I'd seen enough television shows with psychics solving missing person's cases or mediums who could speak to the dead. I liked to believe I had an open mind and didn't automatically assume someone was a charlatan because I didn't possess their sixth sense. But when these same inexplicable experiences affected me directly...I needed to go with the explanation that made me less crazy.

I rolled the last few feet to Drew's door. As usual, he lay on his bed watching television. I tapped on the door. His eyes cut to mine, a snarl curling his lip. "What?" It was soft enough that Margie wouldn't hear him, but cold enough that I knew I wasn't welcome.

Too bad for him I didn't scare that easily. I rolled inside, ignoring his hardened features as he glared at me, his eyes assessing my every move. "Are you always this pleasant or is it just a result of the coma?"

His voice grew a little stronger. "I never said you could come in here."

"Seriously? Because I'm clearly better company than the prodding nurses and over-the-top candy stripers."

His eyes shot back to the television.

Screw that. "Andi."

Drew gave me a sidelong glance. "What?"

"My name. You haven't asked."

He blinked, the motion of his lashes long and drawn out. "Because I don't give a fuck."

My chest constricted. *That son of a bitch.* "Well, it's what normal people do. They introduce themselves, maybe carry on a conversation, get to know each—"

"I've got enough friends."

I twisted around, eyeing the empty doorway. "Yeah, I can see the line."

"Again. I didn't ask you to come in here."

"Again. I'm gonna go with the notion that your coma's the cause of the stick up your ass."

"Nope. Just you."

I threw my head back and laughed, a true, belly-cramping laugh. I liked bantering with him. Liked dishing it back. Liked letting out my frustration at having to start all over with someone I'd already let in. Already developed feelings for. I knew I wasn't crazy. My Drew *was* in there somewhere. This tough, unapproachable guy couldn't be him. I could feel it in the ease of our exchange. No matter how screwed up it was, I could feel it.

"You always talk so much?" he asked.

"Depends. When I'm trying to help a guy who just came out of a coma, yup."

"I already told you how you can help me."

"Yeah. And I probably should've directed you to the gift shop. I'm sure they have magazines under the counter that could help you with that." My eyes flicked to the zipper on his jeans. "See?" I shot him a smug smile. "Help."

"Seriously. What's it gonna take to shut you up?"

"Candy. Lots of it. And good TV." I glanced to the talk show on the screen. "I guess if strippers, home-wreckers, and baby daddies still exist, there's an audience for this, huh?"

Drew didn't respond as I repositioned my chair to get a better angle.

"Which are you?" I asked, more to get a rise out of him than anything else.

He glared at me through tightened eyes.

I purposely dragged my eyes over his athletic body. "By the looks of you, I'd say baby daddy's a strong possibility. Though with your anger issues, I might be swayed to go with home wrecker. Then again, with those muscles and obvious disdain for the spoken word…I'm going with stripper."

Disgust dripped from his snare as he looked back to the television.

With a big smile and a true sense of accomplishment—sad but totally true—I joined him, enduring the ridiculous talk show in silence. While he ignored me, preferring the paternity-test-turned-brawl on the screen to my company, I snuck glances his way. It was crazy. His features were exactly the same. The perfect nose. Full lips. Pronounced cheekbones. How had my hallucinations been so spot-on? So exact?

I expelled a long sigh, mourning the loss of not only my Drew, but my freaking sanity.

"Time for tests, Drew." A pretty young nurse entered the room pushing a wheelchair.

His eyes ignored the overly-friendly nurse, sliding right to his transportation. The anger I'd witnessed firsthand, brewed in his stormy eyes. But he said nothing.

"I guess I'll leave you to it." I grabbed hold of my wheels, reversing slowly. "Thanks for the show."

Drew didn't bother to look at me as I moved to the door, but his nurse did, eyeing me as if she didn't like me being there. I guess post-catatonic state or not, he still had women vying for his attention—or converting to catty bitches.

I made it into the hallway and down the hall to the elevator with thoughts of our latest encounter on my mind. This Drew was a real piece of work, but a small part of me hoped against all hope that I'd been able to chip away a tiny bit of his tough façade. If not, I was just a glutton for punishment, setting myself up for yet another big disappointment.

CHAPTER NINE

I'd finally taken a real shower, with the help of a nurse who covered my cast with enough plastic to conceal a family of four. I felt so much better—fresher, cleaner, less hairy. I'd spent a few minutes on the phone talking to Logan about finals when a knock on my door grabbed my attention.

A good looking guy with dirty blonde hair and scruff along his jawline stood in my doorway.

"I'm gonna have to call you back." I didn't wait for Logan to respond. I disconnected the call and locked eyes with my visitor. "Can I help you?"

An easy smile slid across his face, reaching its way to his honey colored eyes. "I'm Avery."

I stared across the room, wondering why his name sounded so familiar.

"Drew's friend," he clarified.

That's when it clicked. "The supplier."

His brows furrowed.

"The vodka that kicked my ass. You brought it."

He cocked his head. "Vodka?"

Shit.

I shook my head, more to clear the tainted memory than for his benefit. "Never mind."

"Can I come in?"

"Sure." I smiled a little too widely, surprised he'd still want to.

He walked inside, his eyes drawn to the colorful balloons Logan had brought floating by the vent in the corner of the room where I'd tried to hide them.

"I'm a little surprised Drew actually has any friends. He's pretty—"

"Oh, he's definitely pretty." Avery dropped into the chair beside me. "Or so all the girls tell him."

"That's not what I—"

He snickered. "I know. I was just having a little fun with you. But yeah, I assume you were going to point out that he's got a reputation for being pretty hard to handle sometimes."

I shrugged.

"Well, I've known the guy since junior high. You tend to ignore those things when you know someone so well."

"Junior high, huh?"

He nodded. "We both spent our summers here."

"So, you're not from Wilmington?"

He shook his head. "No, but I go to school here and my family's beach house is here. So, it's pretty much my second home."

"Which school?"

"UNC."

I smiled. "Me, too."

"Yeah. I know." He examined my cast for a brief moment. "I heard about your accident."

Of course the whole campus would've known Marley was headed to the Olympics and not me. She'd never been one to keep quiet about anything. And beating the school record-holder, even by default, would've been her biggest feat yet.

"The nurses mentioned you've been stopping by to see Drew." Avery's voice pulled me from my head.

"Seemed like he needed a friend." I omitted the fact that my shrink made me. "And now here you are."

He rested his elbows on his knees and linked his fingers, pausing before meeting my gaze. "Drew's complicated."

"Hard to handle and complicated. Sounds like a great friend."

He raised a brow. "The nurses said you've been back more than once."

"Yeah. For some Godforsaken reason, I feel like there's something else going on underneath the tough exterior. Like, maybe there's a reason he's such an asshole."

Avery's head shot back. "You've talked to him?"

"Um." I swallowed down that damn guilty knot that kept emerging in my throat. I was a terrible liar. But deflector? I could deflect like no one's business. "Have you?"

He cocked his head.

Or not.

"Okay. He talked to me." It gushed out in a single breath.

His eyes grew in amusement. "That son of a bitch."

"You really didn't know?" I actually experienced a tinge of guilt for ratting him out. He obviously had his reasons for not wanting people to know he could talk.

Avery shook his head. "Looks like you're the only one my buddy's been talking to."

"Lucky me."

He studied my face, his eyes lingering on the scratches on my cheek longer than any other area. "Why do you think that is?"

"I'm a total babe?"

He snickered. "No. I'm serious."

I pegged him with my eyes. "So, I'm not a total babe?"

He laughed. "Have you looked in a mirror? Of course you are. But that's not what I meant."

His compliment—fictional as it may have been—earned him a reprieve. "Fine. My guess is he's working an angle."

"An angle?"

I nodded. "In hopes that I'll pleasure him."

He choked out a cough.

I crossed my arms, unsure if he doubted me or thought I wasn't Drew's type. "I'm completely serious. He propositioned me."

"And how exactly did he go about propositioning you?" he asked with a smile in his voice.

"He unbuttoned his shorts and told me it had been awhile."

Avery's shoulders actually relaxed. "Thank God."

My forehead creased and my head whipped back. "Excuse me?"

"No. That came out wrong. I'm not saying him doing that was okay. It just sounds like something he'd do, that's all."

"So he makes a habit out of propositioning girls?"

He shook his head. "He doesn't usually have to. They're usually more than willing."

I felt my arms tightening across my chest and my fists clenching beneath them. It wasn't like the news shocked me. More like repulsed me.

"Let me apologize," Avery continued. "Because nothing justifies him doing that to you."

"Come on, Avery. He's a big boy. He can take responsibility for what comes out of his mouth."

"You're right. But for a long time, he's been given anything his heart desires and things he didn't even think to ask for. People don't say no to Drew Slater. And sometimes, that's a really bad thing. Personally, I think it's why he finds it difficult to trust people and their motives. When it comes to someone he hasn't known his whole life, he has a hard time letting them in. But between you and me, I think he could use another friend."

I couldn't disguise my exasperation. "Then tell him to stop being such a jerk."

"Oh, believe me, that's an ongoing battle." He stood up and smiled down at me. "But maybe you should tell him since you're the only one he's actually talking to."

"Like he's gonna listen to me."

He shrugged. "You never know."

* * *

My newfound cleanliness, a fresh change of clothes, and Avery's visit propelled me downstairs. I wasn't sure if I planned to visit Drew or just check with the nurses to see if he'd spoken. Avery couldn't have been right. I couldn't have been the only person Drew had spoken to.

A breathy female voice inside Drew's room stopped me by the nurses' station across from his room. I waited, pretending to be interested in a genital herpes brochure while I focused my attention on that voice.

"Come on, Drew. Your parents said if anyone could get you talking, it'd be me." A husky laugh followed. One I imagined came from a supermodel's mouth. Drew was too hot not to date one. "I couldn't bear to tell them that you and I never really spent much time talking. That was never our thing. Was it, babe?"

My stomach roiled as I found myself front and center to the life this Drew lived.

I craned my neck, spotting Drew on his bed with his eyes locked on the television. A blonde with loose flowing curls sat in the chair beside him with her long tanned legs crossed. "I bet I know what I can do to get you talking." She stood on chunky wedges and sauntered toward the door as if strutting down the catwalk. She had every right to. She *was* drop-dead gorgeous—and showing more cleavage in her tight white tank top than what she had covered.

Totally called it.

Once the door to his room clicked shut, something struck me. Not the predictability of what would occur behind closed doors. Not the fact that I found myself slightly jealous. But the fact that I was still the only one who he'd spoken to.

* * *

My cheeks prickled in the hot afternoon sun. It was my own fault. I'm the one who decided to slide out of my chair and strand myself on a bench. But my stupid pride stopped me from asking anyone for help.

"Ms. Parker?"

My eyes shot up.

Officer Roy in plain-clothes and a baseball hat eyed the empty space beside me on the bench. "Mind if I sit?"

I shook my head.

The bench strained under his weight. "Sorry it's taken me a while to get back here."

"I didn't realize you'd be back. Seemed like a pretty cut and dry case to me."

He studied my face to an almost uncomfortable degree.

Were my cheeks lobster red? Was my scratch cracking? Was it something else? I couldn't take the not knowing. "What?"

He shook his head, his eyes drifting to the bustling grounds. "Is there any reason someone would have to hurt you?"

My head jerked back. "Hurt me?"

He turned to me, looking me straight in the eyes. "The tire tracks on the sandy road. They were clear as day. There was no indication the driver even attempted to stop."

My brows bunched. "But you said they lost control."

"It's what I said I presumed happened."

"Well did you ask the driver?"

He shook his head. "I needed to ask you first."

To say my mind spun would be an understatement. It was a tornado pulling in houses and spitting them back out with ruthless force. I couldn't focus on a single thought. Too many bombarded my head. Too many faces I'd come across over the years. Too many moments of teenage drama I wished I could erase. Too many exes I'd like to forget.

"I didn't come here to worry you. I just like to cover all my bases—Are you still in school?" His subject change yanked me back to the present.

"I'm graduating from UNC in a few weeks." My words were slow, my mind and body competing for balance.

"Do you work?"

I shook my head. "I run." I glanced down at my cast. "At least I did. I was supposed to be heading to the Olympics this summer."

His head recoiled. "Why didn't you tell me?"

Tell him? "Why does it matter?"

"You're probably too young to remember. But some years ago, two ice skaters were in the news when one allegedly conspired to hurt the other to secure a spot on the Olympic team." He glanced to my cast. "Kind of ironic, don't you think?"

My eyes shot around as I fought to make sense of what he'd suggested. "So, you think the driver was doing someone else's dirty work?"

He shrugged.

Fuuuck.

I considered who would've benefited from my being hurt. Those I'd outrun. Those who rubbed me the wrong way. Those I rubbed the wrong way. It seemed so far-fetched. People actually conspiring to hurt me. But there I sat. Broken bones and torn ligaments to prove it.

I begrudgingly gave him two names, Marley and another girl who'd often finished tenths of a second behind me. I hoped to God—after throwing them under the bus—they had nothing to do with it.

"I'll look into their whereabouts at the time of the accident. Or any other evidence that could link them to it." Sensing my unease, he gave me a fatherly look. "There are a lot of people out there willing to do whatever it takes to be in the position you were slated to be in."

I nodded. I didn't know an Olympic hopeful who hadn't dreamt of landing the coveted sport's drink commercial or cereal box cover. But hurting someone to make it a reality, when that someone was me, stung like nothing else.

Officer Roy helped me back into my chair before heading back to the station. I opted to stay outside, the fresh air easing my frazzled brain. He must've felt sorry for delivering such bad news—or I really did look like a lobster—because he left me his hat and made me wear it, making me promise to stay out of the sun.

Had someone tried to hurt me? Had I really been a target when all along I believed it was some freak accident? I hated thinking people I knew, girls I'd competed with, could've planned something so devious. So hurtful. So selfish. Yet there I sat. Incapable of running. Incapable of competing. Incapable of winning a medal.

A short time later, visons of my bed carried me back toward the building. I needed to lose myself in my dreams and hope they weren't anything like my living nightmare. I rolled to the sliding doors I used to exit the building, but when I stopped in front of them, they didn't open. Were they broken? Locked for the night?

My head whipped around, realizing my only option was the main entrance on the other side of the building. *Fan-freaking-tastic.* I made my way slowly around, giving my arms an unexpected workout. When I rounded the corner, I stopped short. Television cameras sat aimed at the front doors. Photographers with long-lensed cameras around their necks paced. Reporters with phones to their ears spoke animatedly. Others held their phones in their palms with their eyes glued to them.

"What's going on?" I asked a man standing off to the side.

He didn't even bother looking up from the phone in his hand. "A big shot football hopeful's inside."

"And that's news?"

"When he's supposed to be the number one draft pick, and now no one knows if he'll even be able to enter the draft, yeah. It's a big deal." He finally looked up. "Surprised you didn't know. Women seem to love the guy. Nothing like a wounded athlete to get them all hot, bothered, and buying magazines."

I nodded, wishing those women knew what their good-looking football star was really like.

Once I'd cleared the small crowd, I made my way over to the elevator. I pressed the button and watched the red glowing numbers until the car reached the lobby. When the doors slid apart, I rolled forward.

"Watch it," a voice growled.

My eyes shot up from under Officer Roy's hat. Drew's cold face glared down at me. I shook my head in complete and utter disgust. How could he be some different from the Drew I fabricated? "God, you're such a prick."

He didn't move. "What did you call me?"

I held his cold glare. "A prick."

"Bitch."

"That's original."

He stared at me long and hard. A mixture of anger and exhaustion clouded those once pretty eyes. It had clearly taken a lot of effort for him to get himself downstairs. But, of course, the stubborn ass wouldn't take a wheelchair.

"Well, go ahead." I swept out my arm. "Don't let me stop you. Get wherever you were going. Maybe try the front door. Seems like a lot of fun out there." *Asshole*.

His eyes narrowed, but he didn't budge.

I huffed out my annoyance. "I've got no interest in whatever game you're playing. I'm tired and just found out someone tried to kill me. So, yeah, I win."

He blinked hard. I assumed my words had struck a chord because he stepped aside to let me enter.

Moving forward, I jabbed my finger into the number five button. I spun my chair around, jolting back when Drew stepped beside me as the doors sealed us alone inside.

We waited in silence as the elevator ascended. He was delusional if he thought I'd let his presence bother me any more than I already was. But I still wished I was on my feet so I could move into the far corner, as far from him as I could get. I was sick and tired of being dumped on…by the world.

The elevator stopped on the second floor and the doors slid apart. As if the ride wasn't awkward enough, no one waited to get on. I could hear Drew's heavy sigh as the doors closed and the car ascended. Still, I wouldn't look at him standing there, a foot away, towering over me in my chair. No matter how silent the car was. No matter how much tension existed in that small space. He would not get that.

The car stopped on the third floor. Again, no one waited.

Damn button-pushing kids.

The doors shut, leaving us to more torturous silence. Eventually, they split on the fourth floor. I expected Drew to step off and leave me alone, but he remained still and the doors closed again.

"Why would someone want to hurt you?" His deep voice tore through the silence.

I forced my eyes to him. "My big mouth?"

"I'm serious." His eyes cut to mine. "Why would someone purposely hurt you?"

"I don't know. Why are *you* always purposely hurting me?"

It was as though I'd slapped him across the face. His head flinched and his eyes darted away. I could've cut the silence with a sharp object, or at least stabbed Drew with it.

A sense of relief washed over me as we stopped on my floor and the doors split. Drew shot me a slanted look. His way of asking for the true answer to his question.

I rolled forward and called out without looking back. "Long story."

"I've got nowhere to be."

I glanced over my shoulder. He stood with one foot on my floor and one foot in the elevator, stopping the doors from closing. "That's not how it looked downstairs."

He buried his hands in his pockets. "So, you're not gonna tell me?"

I stared into the eyes of a guy I wished was someone else. Someone sincere. Someone I could rely on. Someone who claimed to know me. But now I could see. That just wasn't him. "You should probably go sit down. You're not looking so good." I tore my eyes away and grabbed hold of my wheels, rolling away without bothering to glance back.

He stayed on the elevator.

And that was fine by me.

CHAPTER TEN

"What are you doing this weekend?"

Logan's eyes flashed up from the foot of my bed where she painted hot pink polish onto my toenails. "Well, remember Luke from my sociology class last year?"

"The one who never called?"

She nodded.

"He called." It wasn't a question. She wouldn't have brought it up had he not. She wasn't one to sulk or complain. Especially over a guy.

She nodded again.

"He waited long enough."

She laughed. "Tell me about it. But he doesn't live around here. If things go well—which of course they will since this is me we're talking about—he'll be gone all summer."

Her overconfidence never failed to amuse me. "Maybe you and your big head are enough of a reason for him to stick around."

"Maybe?" she asked playfully aghast. "Honey. I'm the total package."

I laughed. "I'm serious. If he can't stay—for whatever reason—then at least you'll have a couple good weeks before he leaves. Give the guy a break. He watched tons of guys fall victim to your player ways. Who can blame him for not wanting to be tossed to the side for the next big thing?"

A sly smile swept across her glossy lips. "Big thing?"

"Yeah, walked right into that one, didn't I?"

Logan nodded. "But so you know, I don't toss them to the side. I release them back to the masses."

"You're a bitch, you know that right?"

"Takes one to know one. And don't be fooled," she twisted the cap back onto the polish. "Guys love it. Maybe that's what Drew needs."

I scoffed. "I don't think Drew knows what Drew needs."

"Come on." Logan stood up. "Given the recent developments, let me roll you down to the cafeteria before I head back to campus."

I furrowed my brows. "Recent developments?"

"Someone trying to off you."

I shook my head, unsure if she truly believed I was in danger.

"This way, not only are you protected, but you can show off these hot nails."

Logan left me alone at a corner table. But instead of facing the table or the room, she spun me so my chair faced the floor to ceiling windows overlooking the grounds. Apparently she wasn't *that* worried about me. She left me an easy target for any trained sharp-shooter. Scratch that. Any kid with a BB gun could likely pull off the job.

Then again, with two bum legs, no one had any reason to get rid of me now.

I sat for a long time gazing out the windows. Patients walked around admiring the beautiful landscapes. Visitors bustled in and out of the building. Nurses chatted on benches while eating lunch.

Life certainly didn't stop. It kept moving and expected all of us to do the same. But would I ever be able to move the way I once had? Would I ever be able to get back out on the track? Would I ever be the person I once was? Or would my life be forever changed by this massive setback?

"This food sucks," a deep voice muttered.

My ponytail slapped me in the face as my head whipped around.

Drew slipped his food tray onto my table and dropped into the seat across from me, keeping his back to the room.

Avoiding reporters and groupies must've been a full time job.

"What I wouldn't give for a big greasy pizza," he muttered, looking just as exhausted as the previous day.

My belly dipped at the mention of pizza. Did he remember something? Was he testing me? I rotated my chair so I faced the table—and could get a better look at him. "My roommate had one delivered."

I watched him closely as he lifted his burger and took a bite, his eyes never meeting mine.

"Not sure where he got it, but he called it cheesy goodness. And it was." Not wanting to face the fact that this jackass was really him, I tried jogging his memory, searching for the slightest bit of familiarity.

"Where'd he go?" he asked with his mouthful.

I shrugged. "One day he was here, the next he was gone without so much as a goodbye."

He stared at me across the table as he swallowed down his bite. "Sounds like a douche."

I choked out a laugh. I'd wanted us to be face to face. I'd wanted to see even the slightest resemblance to the guy I knew. I'd wanted to see the Drew that his friend saw. I'd wanted to see if that pull still existed between us. But now that he sat across from me, a mere two feet away, it was as if oceans separated us. And I just needed to be okay with that. "So, how are you feeling?"

He shrugged, taking another bite of his burger.

I reached across the table and stole a couple fries from his plate. "Does anyone know you can talk yet?"

He shook his head.

"Why not?"

He wiped his mouth with a napkin and looked up at me. "Because then I'd have to answer a million fucking questions."

I looked out across the bustling room. No one could accuse me of not taking a hint. "I can't believe I'm gonna say this. But I know what it's like to be stuck in this place alone. So I'm here if you need someone to talk to."

I could hear the surprise in his voice. "You don't even know me."

I forced my eyes back to him. "Oh, I know you all right."

Instead of smiling, like the other Drew would've, his face hardened. "Comments like that aren't convincing me you're not a reporter."

My brows scrunched together. "First of all, *you* sat down with me. And second, do you seriously think the broken leg, torn ACL, and wheelchair are my cover? *Really?*"

He shrugged.

"Why is it you think you have reporters and groupies following you around anyway?" No way I'd confess I knew who he was. Plus, I was becoming increasingly pissed off.

He said nothing.

"Okay. Then let me guess." I tapped my bottom lip, totally working my acting chops. If he was going to continue to be a jerk, I was going to have a little fun. "You're some hotshot racecar driver. No." I held up my index finger. "A country music singer. I could totally picture you rocking the cowboy boots."

He tilted his head, studying my features for a long moment. From my eyes, to my scratched cheek, to my lips, he took in every inch like he'd never actually taken the time to do so before. That, or he had absolutely no idea what to make of me.

Hell, *I* didn't know what to make of me. I could've been sitting alone at a table talking to myself for all I knew. "Okay. Maybe not a singer. How about an actor? No, wait. I know. An MMA fighter."

"Quarterback."

My stomach quivered. Even though the reporter had already confirmed the fact, it still baffled my mind that my hallucinations had been so accurate. If he and my Drew shared that, maybe they shared other things, too. As unlikely as it seemed, the possibility did exist. "Where?"

"Duke."

I shook out my arms, feigning chills—all the while celebrating yet another similarity. "I shudder at the mention of Blue Devils. I go to UNC."

I could have sworn his lips twitched. "So you have no idea who I am?"

"Sorry to disappoint."

His eyes lowered. "Well, that's refreshing."

"I have been known to be refreshing, among other things. None of which is a groupie who wants to drop to her knees for you, though."

He averted his gaze in what could only be described as embarrassment. Nice to know he wasn't as impenetrable as he would've liked everyone to believe.

I needed to maintain the upper hand. It seemed to work in the elevator because here he sat. So I reached down and gripped my wheels. "See you around." I moved away from the table and rolled away without another word.

I'd leave on my terms.

And he and his ego would be just fine.

CHAPTER ELEVEN

I'd spent the following day typing a finance essay my business professor sent as a take-home exam. Once I hit send, a small weight lifted from my shoulders. I was one step closer to graduating. That called for a celebration.

I'd teased Drew about the gift shop's assortment of gentlemen's magazines, but I wasn't far off. They had everything you could think of—including endless jars of penny-candy.

"For someone confined to a wheelchair, you really think all that sugar's a good idea?" Drew's voice carried over from somewhere nearby.

My hand literally dangled in the gummy worms jar. To be totally obnoxious, I grabbed a handful and shoved them into my mouth. When I glanced over my shoulder, I made sure some hung out, and then sucked them in like a little kid eating spaghetti.

His eyes zoned in on my mouth. And the disgust I thought I'd garner was replaced by something else. Something I'd never seen in this Drew's eyes. Desire.

WTF?

"I'm sure the girl I saw in your room the other day wouldn't be caught dead ingesting more than ten calories a day." I chomped offensively on the chewy candy. "But have you seen me? I'm a hundred pounds soaking wet. I can handle a little sugar."

Drew forced his eyes up to mine, the look disappearing. "It's your life."

"Yup. It is." I rolled over to the cashier. She weighed my candy bag then handed it back. I held it out toward Drew as she swiped my credit card. "I dare you."

He eyed the bag. Then his eyes shot to mine.

"You know you want to. All that sugary goodness."

He stared down at the bag for a long moment. You'd think he was an alcoholic and I'd offered him a drink. Before I realized what he was doing, he'd ripped the bag out of my hand and dug in. I resisted the urge to smirk as he stole a few pieces before handing it back to me and stuffing the pieces into his mouth. He grabbed hold of my chair and pushed me out of the gift shop.

What the? "Really, I'm fine."

"Nope. I've got it."

Short of throwing a tantrum or yelling "Help," there really wasn't anything I could do to stop him, so I let him push me through the lobby. "Where are we going?"

"To get some fresh air."

"Were you following me?"

He balked as my chair cleared the sliding doors, and he walked me outside, avoiding the main entrance with its persistent reporters.

"Seems pretty coincidental that we both ended up in the gift shop at the same time. Don't you think?"

"Not really. I hate being in my room," he admitted. "I walk around a lot."

"You do realize you just came out of a coma, right? From everything I've read, you shouldn't be able to do that."

"Yet, here I am."

"One of life's little miracles."

He snickered. I so wished he wasn't behind me. I would've loved to see it. Loved to see any change in his cold features. Did he show his teeth or that cocky smirk my Drew had perfected? Did his eyes dance playfully or smolder?

"So, no Busty Betty today?" I asked, trying to keep our conversation light.

He choked out a laugh. "Busty Betty?"

"You know who I'm talking about."

He sighed behind me. "Yeah. I've got lots of those in my past."

"Strippers?"

"She's not a stripper—at least I don't think she is." He stopped me beside the bench we shared—in another lifetime—and dropped onto it.

I dragged in a long breath, hating all the unwelcome moments of déjà vu. "She's not your girlfriend?"

He shook his head. "No girlfriend."

"Yeah. Probably should've guessed. You're way too much of a pain in the ass."

His lips quirked. "Is that so?"

"Girls like a laid back guy. You are the complete opposite of laid back."

His head recoiled. "I know plenty of girls who don't mind."

"Besides Busty, I haven't noticed any of them here."

His eyes drifted away.

I should've been happy to have knocked him down a peg or two, but I suddenly felt like shit for being insensitive. I wasn't him. I didn't purposely set out to hurt other people. *Rewind.* "So, since you've made a full recovery and all, when do you think they'll be releasing you?"

He shrugged. "Trying to get rid of me?"

"Damn straight."

He laughed. Like a real laugh. Deep and raspy. The kind that reaches all the way down to the toes of anyone lucky enough to hear it.

Well, that's refreshing. And about freaking time.

A little girl with pigtails chased an older man along the path. When they neared us, she stumbled. Drew jumped up and helped her to her feet. She smiled up at him with a giant gap where her front teeth should've been. "Thanks."

He tugged gently on her pigtails. "No sweat, kid."

I tried not to melt at the small exchange, but for some reason every fiber of my being longed to touch him. To make him remember me. Remember the fun we'd had. Remember the possibilities that existed between us.

He settled back onto the bench and reached into my candy bag as the little girl trotted off. We watched patients, visitors, and staff cross the busy lawn like two people who shared more than just a bag of candy. But truthfully, that's all we were.

"I haven't noticed you with any visitors either." Drew didn't bother to look at me. His eyes followed the little girl as she zigzagged across the lawn with the man now tailing her.

"Didn't realize you were paying attention."

"You walk around here long enough, you notice things."

I turned toward him, though his eyes didn't waver. "Should I be concerned you're roaming the dark halls late at night?"

"I'm a big boy. I can take care of myself."

I laughed. "I was talking about me and the other people you're stalking. It's a little creepy."

He chuckled low in his throat, reining back his laughter for some reason.

"Well, just so you know…" I lowered my voice, as if to let him in on a huge secret. "I plan on locking my door from now on."

He smiled, a friendly, easy smile. "You don't think I know how to sweet talk the nurses into letting me in?"

I narrowed my eyes. "First of all, sweet talking requires actually *talking* to them. Second, why would you need to get into my room? I already explained your…" My eyes shot to his zipper. "Situation has nothing to do with me."

"I'm never gonna live that down, am I?"

I shook my head. "Oh, no. That one was a real doozy."

"Doozy? What are you my grandmother?"

I laughed at his amusement. "Nope, you wouldn't have made her the offer."

He snickered. "Yeah…I can be a real asshole sometimes."

"Sometimes?"

He laughed, actually allowing himself to let go. He sounded so much like the old Drew.

My traitorous heart did a little flip. I needed to put a stop to that. Immediately. "You asked about my visitors. My best friend Logan tries to stop by every day. It's my parents who don't. They're out of the country."

His eyes finally cut to mine. "Where are they?"

"Saving whales."

His eyes grew wide with intrigue. "No shit?"

"I shit you not."

"Like that television show where smaller boats go up against those giant whaling vessels?"

I nodded. "I don't watch. It makes me too nervous."

He shook his head in disbelief. "Talk about balls. That right there gets fucking crazy."

"My parents are more of the peaceful protesters," I explained, more for my own benefit and reassurance than for him.

"You said your friend tries to stop by," he probed, seemingly interested in what I had to say.

"She'd be here more if she wasn't cramming for finals. She really needs to pass seeing as though she nearly flunked out freshmen year and isn't graduating with me as it is."

"You're graduating?" he asked, as if the notion had never crossed his mind.

I nodded. "On the twentieth."

"Yeah? Me, too."

The other Drew hadn't mentioned Duke graduated the same day as UNC. "Are you feeling up to taking your finals?"

He reached into the bag and pulled out a couple gummy worms. "My professors already sent take-homes."

"One of the perks of being an athlete?"

"One of the perks of being the *star* athlete." He wasn't bragging. Just the opposite. He was put-off by the notion.

"A true golden boy, huh? Am I required to bow down?"

"Fuck off."

I smiled. "Need I remind you? You're the one who followed me."

He stuffed one of the worms into his mouth. "In your dreams."

"Nope. Can't say I've seen you there." Too often.

His head tilted to the side, doubt dancing in his eyes. *Bastard.*

"So what's your plan when you get out of here?" I asked.

His eyes narrowed, his words hesitant, almost distrustful. "What do you mean?"

I shrugged. "Your plans after you graduate." Down deep, I wondered if playing pro football remained a possibility, as it had for the other Drew. Or if this Drew was just as opposed to it. But how could I broach the subject without bringing up a potentially sore subject *or* divulging I knew more than I was letting on?

"I'm not really sure," he admitted. "I'll have my physical therapy degree. But I'll still need to take my Boards."

My head withdrew. "That's what you want to do?"

He nodded. "Quite a few miracle workers got me back on the field after injuries. I want to pay if forward." He must've seen the admiration in my eyes because he said no more.

Maybe there was more to this Drew than the tough façade. The intolerance. The callousness.

"How about you?" His eyes remained on mine.

"How ironic would it be if I said reporter?"

He shot me a dubious grin.

"I don't really know. I was supposed to make it to the Olympics." My bottom lip jutted out in contemplation. "Now, I have no clue."

"The Olympics?" He sounded shocked, like he hadn't heard me droning on about it in his hospital room when he wasn't speaking. "For what?"

I glanced to my legs. "800 meter track."

"Fuuuuck."

"Yup."

I wasn't sure he'd say anything else. I mean, really? What was there to say? But he did. "So what now?"

I shrugged. "No idea. My backup plan sucks."

"Why's that?"

I looked to him. "My coach taught me to focus solely on the medal, not what came next. He said it would take away from everything I was striving to do."

Drew nodded, seemingly understanding.

"So. Any idea what a business major who never wanted to be a business major does now?"

"I guess anything you set your mind to."

"Yeah." My voice drifted off as I gazed out at the lightly swaying trees. "What if that's running?"

"Then you do that."

My eyes dropped to my legs. "You make it sound easy."

"Nope. Not easy. But you've got guts."

My eyes jumped to his. "Says who?"

He shrugged. "Sounded like something encouraging to say."

I threw back my head and laughed. A refreshing, shoulder-shaking, eyes-watering laugh. I let it all out—the frustration, the anger, the loneliness—and it felt incredible. And even better knowing Drew caused it. "You were trying to be encouraging?"

He fought back a smile. "Maybe."

"Wow. That's quite a stretch from an asshole."

He snickered as steely clouds moved in, covering the sun.

A light chill sent a shiver surging through me. But for once, I wasn't in a rush to get away from him. We sat in companionable silence watching tiny leaves blow across the property as patients and visitors gradually dispersed inside the building.

I'd be lying if I said knowing what brought on Drew's coma hadn't been on my mind. His frequent mood swings and split personalities were enough to give anyone whiplash. Had the coma caused it, or was he really that way? Avery confirmed he was difficult. But did I risk asking Drew about it and potentially setting him off, bringing back the cold Drew? Was it really that important to know? Right now?

"Want to get some lunch?" Drew's voice tugged me from my indecision.

I looked to him, surprised by the unexpected invitation. "My candy wasn't good enough?"

He leveled me with his eyes. "Not if you want to get back out on the track."

"So, you're worried about me?"

He shrugged. "You worry about me."

"Worry's not the right word," I mused. "Tolerate. Endure. Empathize with maybe."

Drew's eyes darkened, his features hardened, and a nasty scowl bent his lips. "I don't need your fucking pity."

My entire body jerked back. "What?"

As if the last few minutes never happened, he jumped to his feet. "I don't know why I even bothered."

"*You* bothered?" I growled, finding it difficult to rein back my anger.

"Yeah." He shook his head. "What a mistake."

My jaw hung open. "Are you freaking kidding me? I'm the one who's been enduring the bulk of your bullshit since I'm the only one you actually talk to!" My knuckles whitened as I gripped my knees. "If anyone shouldn't have bothered, it should've been me!"

Anyone still mulling around turned our way.

"If I didn't have a cast on my leg right now, I'd be the one leaving, you asshole!" My eyes shot away and my entire body trembled.

Without a word, Drew turned around and took off toward the building.

"I hate you!" I yelled at his retreating form, like the nut I'd undoubtedly become.

No. Like the nut he was making me.

CHAPTER TWELVE

I stared down at my hairy right leg which I hadn't seen in weeks. And except for Doctor Evans, who'd just removed my cast, no one else would be seeing it until I had a very lengthy date with a well sharpened razor.

"How's it feel?"

I wiggled my toes before slightly bending my knee. "Stiff."

He nodded. "It'll take time. But you're an athlete. Athletes, especially determined ones, make the best rehab patients. They do the work so they can get back out there. Just know, it won't be better overnight. You still need to wear a boot to keep it stabilized. I don't want you thinking it's one-hundred percent yet."

"I understand."

"Tomorrow you start therapy in our rehab facility. Your new therapist will give you range of motion exercises for both your knee and leg. He'll also get you on crutches so you won't be bound to that wheelchair."

"Thank God."

He laughed. "Based on his assessment, and of course Doctor Fallon's concurrence, we'll start looking at discharging you."

I couldn't contain my smile. "Thank you."

"Don't thank me yet. You still need to do the work."

I nodded, certain I'd do whatever it took to get me home and walking again.

* * *

I arrived at the therapy room the following day. What I didn't expect to find when I wheeled inside the state-of-the-art facility was a good looking blonde not much older than me helping a gray-haired woman on a stationary bike.

When he spotted me in the doorway, a smile spread across his face. "You must be Andi."

I nodded. *Hello, blue eyes.*

"Well, come in. Mary and I were just finishing up."

I glanced to Mary. Her legs pedaled away on her bike while her eyes checked out his ass like she wanted to take a bite out of it. I couldn't blame her. His jeans sat low on his hips and hugged it like no one's business.

"I'm Anthony." He approached with an outstretched hand. "I hope you're ready to sweat."

My eyes went wide, my mind embarrassingly inundated with impure thoughts.

"And get rid of that chair," Anthony clarified.

I nodded, shaking his firm grip and clearing my mind of any sweat-related images. "Absolutely."

Anthony might've been hot, but he didn't take it easy on me. If anything, he pushed me too hard for my first go at it. I'd spent a long hour stretching and attempting range of motion exercises I worried would re-tear my ACL or re-snap my fragile bones. By the end of our session, my knee and leg throbbed incessantly, but everything was still intact. A disgusting sheen of sweat covered my face. My T-shirt and shorts clung to my body like I'd jumped fully-clothed into a pool.

But something about Anthony's calm voice and relaxed demeanor put me at ease. Okay. So maybe it was his blue eyes that put me at ease. I was such a sucker for pretty eyes.

I reclined on the massage table on the verge of drifting off to sleep as Anthony's thumbs pressed into the arch of my foot. My eyes literally rolled into the back of my head. His cool-down massage was *that* good.

"Do all your patients get this treatment or just the pretty ones?"

My eyes snapped open. Drew stood in the doorway with his arms crossed over his chest, his eyes shooting daggers at Anthony.

Anthony paid him no attention, continuing to work wonders on my foot. "What's up, Slater?"

So they knew each other.

Drew's hardened mask never faltered. "Are you almost done?"

I stared across the room for a long moment before realizing his question was directed at me. "What?"

He threw out his hand. "This. You just about done here?"

Was this an alternate reality? Why did he care if I was done? Hadn't we said all that needed to be said?

Anthony didn't even bother looking at him. He just moved his hands to my other foot. "The perk of Andi being *my* patient is I get to say when she's done."

"That's how it's gonna be then?" Drew asked.

Again unsure who his words were meant for, I looked to him. His eyes were glued on Anthony's hands on my foot.

Then, as if he'd never even been there, he tore his eyes away and walked off.

"From what I heard, the guy couldn't talk yet," Anthony said.

I looked down at him crouched at my feet. "Are you gonna tell me what that was about?"

A smile stretched across his face. "We know each other."

"No shit."

He snickered. "Drew was a year behind me at Duke, but we were in the same PT program."

"He told me that was his major."

"Yeah, well, he was the hot shot football player who got everything he wanted. Everything except the coveted summer internship."

"Let me guess. You got it?"

He shrugged. "Some people get things handed to them on a silver platter. Some of us have to work for what we get. That was a life lesson for Drew. One he didn't take well. Especially since I got to teach it to him."

"That's it?"

"That...and I dated his ex."

I laughed. "I knew there had to be more."

He grinned. "Hey. The guy goes through girls like he goes through jock straps. Someone had to comfort the ones tossed to the side."

I shook my head, remembering a similar conversation with Logan.

"Obviously, I'm not a fan." He lifted his chin toward the now empty doorway. "But that right there was him staking his claim."

I wiped the sweat from my face with the sleeve of my T-shirt. "Hardly. We can barely even tolerate each other."

He quirked a knowing brow. "Well, just be careful."

No kidding.

After therapy, I rolled down the first floor hallway en route to the elevator, desperately needing a shower.

"You got your cast off?"

My head whipped to my left. Drew leaned against the wall with his arms crossed. I glared at him. "Observant."

"How's it feel?" The concern in his voice completely contradicted everything that happened the other day.

I bit my tongue, suppressing what I really wanted to say. I wouldn't be the one to fight. That was his M.O., not mine. "Better without the cast. But sore."

He nodded like he understood. "You should really get some rest. And be sure to elevate it."

I stared at him dumbstruck. "That's what I was headed to do." Was this the same guy who flaked on me the other day? The same guy who told me he shouldn't have bothered talking to me?

Yup. Same green eyes. Same split personalities.

When I made to move forward, he motioned with his head back toward the therapy room. "You two looked chummy."

"He's nice. And a good therapist."

Drew scoffed, his concerned disposition quickly fading.

My eyes narrowed. "What's it to you anyway?"

He shrugged, the coolness returning to his eyes. "Just calling it like I see it."

I couldn't stop my eyes from rolling. "Well, the way I *see it*, it's really none of your business. You lost that privilege the second you went all crazy on me." I shook my head, done playing his game—whatever it was. "From here on out, I promise to stay away from you. Just do the same for me." I pushed my wheels and rolled off leaving him a distant memory.

Or at least trying to.

I couldn't exactly ignore his growl or the sound of his fist slamming into the wall as I disappeared around the corner.

* * *

The next day, Anthony positioned me against the massage table while he fit me for my crutches. Once the rubber armrests sat under my armpits, I balanced. At least I endeavored to. It was no easy feat with a boot on my right foot and my recovering left leg needed for support.

"Try to make a lap around the room," Anthony urged.

My first attempt was awkward. It wasn't easy getting into a natural rhythm, putting the crutches in front before swinging myself to meet them. After numerous uncomfortable attempts, I began to get the hang of it and made my way around the room feeling more unrestrained than I had in weeks.

"You're doing great," Anthony called as I picked up speed, circling the room like a woman on a mission.

I couldn't help the laughter that erupted from deep within me. Freedom felt near. I could practically taste it.

"Hey, slow down before you fall," Anthony called out amused.

"I can't," I managed between laughter. "I feel so freeeeee." That's when I caught sight of Drew standing in the doorway with a small smile on his face. As soon as our gazes collided, his smile faded.

The unexpected distraction caused me to falter on my crutches and nearly topple over. When I regained my balance, I glanced back to an empty doorway.

I left Anthony a little while later still in my wheelchair. He worried I'd take off on my crutches and injure myself. And since he'd promised to discharge me after tomorrow's session, and Doctor Fallon had already given her approval, I wouldn't dare risk it.

"Looked like you were having fun in there." Like the previous day, Drew stood against the hallway wall. His eyes hid something I couldn't quite decipher and his hands sat buried in his pockets. I wondered if he'd broken any fingers in his fit of rage.

"What can I say?" I shrugged. "Anthony's fun." I kept rolling. When I didn't hear footsteps, I breathed a sigh of relief. I stopped in front of the elevator, waiting for an older couple to step off. Once they did, I began to roll inside. But something stopped me from moving forward. Like *literally* stopped me from moving. My head flew over my shoulder. Drew gripped my chair, pulling me back and away from the elevator. "What the hell are you doing?"

He said nothing.

Anger boiled inside me as he pushed me through the crowded lobby. There was only one reason I remained quiet and let him push me outside into the cloudy afternoon. I needed to see him. I needed to look into his cold eyes when I exploded on him.

When he reached the closest bench, he stopped and sat down.

"What do you want from me?" I spat.

"Why don't you ever laugh like that with me?"

WTF?

"*Why?*" I shook my head in utter disbelief. "Because you constantly act like a jerk."

He looked away, his eyes taking in everything but me. "Am I that bad to be around?"

I stared at him dumbfounded. *And I'm supposed to be the crazy one?* "Um, yeah. And add your split personalities to the mix, and you're a damn nightmare."

His eyes cut back to mine. Darkness flashed in his expression.

Bring it. I was so ready for him.

He opened his mouth to respond. Then closed it.

"Make up your mind, Drew. Either hate me or don't. You can't have it both ways." I could feel my anger and exasperation growing with every word. "I'm not your punching bag. I don't deserve it. And honestly, I can't take it anymore."

I expected anger, but found only regret in his eyes. He opened his mouth to respond.

"Drew?" a woman called.

Our eyes shot to the voice. Drew's mother crossed the lawn, approaching us hesitantly. Once she stood before us, her words were timid, guarded even. "I was hoping you'd like a visitor."

"Great," I interrupted with a disingenuous smile. "I was just leaving."

Drew's eyes flew to mine, pleading with me to stay.

I leaned closer to him, whispering for only his ears. "Gotta earn a save."

I grasped my wheels, attempting a quick getaway, but Mrs. Slater's voice stopped me.

"How's he doing?" She sat down beside him on the bench.

I shrugged. "You'll have to be the judge of that. I barely know your son." With that, I rolled off, leaving them to work out their own issues.

That's if he decided to talk to her.

* * *

"You're ready," Anthony said as I made my way around the therapy room the following day.

I stopped in my tracks, wiping the sweat from my face with my favorite green T-shirt. "Are you serious?"

He nodded. "I see no reason to keep you here any longer."

My head fell back and I closed my eyes, elation sweeping over my entire body. "Oh, thank God."

"Elite Therapy is one of the best out-patient clinics in the state. Just promise me you'll continue giving it your all."

My eyes popped open. "Absolutely."

A couple hours later, after filling out a stack of paperwork, I was discharged. Since Logan was in the middle of taking an exam, one of my nurses wheeled me down to the lobby to wait for a taxi. The reporters had finally departed. I wondered if it had been on their own accord or if they'd been escorted off the premises. Maybe Drew finally gave them the story they so desperately sought.

My taxi pulled to the curb a few minutes later. I grabbed the plastic bag with my belongings from the floor beside me and hooked it onto the arm of the chair. I leaned down and grabbed my crutches, laying them across my lap. Tasting freedom, I grabbed the wheels and rolled forward only to be stopped by someone grasping my chair. Again.

My head whipped around.

Drew stood staring down at me with an unfathomable expression. "You're leaving?" He sounded appalled.

My eyes dropped to his hands on my wheelchair. "Trying to." I could feel both my voice and anger rising. "Let go of my chair."

He didn't.

"I swear to God—"

Completely ignoring my potential rant, he pushed me outside.

I had lost all patience. "You don't make any sense!"

He stopped at the taxi's back door.

"What's wrong with you?" I shouted.

He released my chair and raked his fingers through his hair. The look in his eyes was wild. Like his world was spiraling out of control. "You!" he shouted back.

"Me?" I couldn't tell if anger or shock laced my voice. Probably both.

"I can't stop fucking thinking about you!"

My breath left me in a giant whoosh. "What?"

He dropped his hands and yanked open the taxi's back door. He leaned in, saying something to the driver I couldn't hear. Then he turned back to me, his eyes avoiding mine as he lifted my crutches and stood them up.

That was it?

He expected to admit something like that and then just send me on my way?

I pushed myself to my feet, balancing on the crutches just enough to hobble into the taxi. I turned, giving him one last chance to explain himself—explain why he'd said such a thing—but he'd already turned to grab my bag from my chair.

Instead of handing it to me when he turned back, he bent down and tried to get in.

I didn't move. "What are you doing?"

"What's it look like? I'm getting in."

"Why?"

At that point, it was either be sat on or move over, so I moved over. He slid inside, and the taxi pulled away from the curb with the two of us seated inside.

My heart began to pound in every part of my body. What in the world was he doing? It was official. *He* was the crazy one. And apparently, I was just along for the insane ride. I didn't look at him. And I didn't speak. No *way* would I speak. This was all him. He was the one who'd jumped inside my taxi. The one who'd made the out-of-left-field declaration. The one who'd lost his ever-loving mind.

He turned his body toward me, breaking the awkward silence. "Do you trust me?"

"Trust you? Why would I trust you? You've lost your freaking skull."

His eyes dropped to his lap. An internal war clearly raged within him as he worked to rein back his temper.

That bought me time. Time to slow down the thoughts racing through my mind. Time to bite back the words teetering on the tip of my tongue. Had I totally misread everything between us? Had I created another fictional situation in my head? But how? Since he'd woken up, he'd made his feelings toward me blatantly clear—on more than one occasion.

Drew's eyes flashed up. "I want to take you somewhere."

"Take me somewhere? Are your meds making you crazy?"

"I'm not on meds," he answered matter-of-factly.

"Is this about Anthony?"

He shook his head. "This is about you and me."

"I didn't realize there was a you and me."

"Then you haven't been paying attention."

See? Split personalities.

I huffed out my frustration. My confusion. My anger. "I'm disgusting. I need a shower."

A subtle smirk lifted the corners of his lips. "I might be able to help with that."

CHAPTER THIRTEEN

"My parents never show up here until after Memorial Day." Drew unscrewed a bottle of soda and handed it to me on the patio lounge chair where he'd left me moments before.

"You got any rum?" I needed something strong to get me through whatever this was.

"That won't help you on your crutches," he advised, like the PT he endeavored to be.

"I think you're forgetting you left them inside after kidnapping me."

He looked at me with a small smile on his face. "I didn't kidnap you."

I glanced to my bare legs. "Taking my crutches and boot ensures I can't go anywhere. That constitutes kidnapping."

His laughter was the only response I got.

I looked out at his family's private beach stretched out before us. The ocean air mixing with the sweet smell of sand brought me back to days when I could run along the coast truly consumed by it. Today, the waves crashed roughly on the shore with the impending storm. Much like the current state of my thrashing heart.

Why was I here?

As if he hadn't made a startling enough confession minutes before, he sat down on the chair beside me. I tried ignoring the questions itching to burst out of me by focusing on the waves, but when he reached over his shoulder and tugged his T-shirt over his head, the pull to peek at the deep ridges and ripples in his abs as he lay back overwhelmed me.

He might've been an ass, but he was still a drop dead gorgeous ass.

I tried refocusing. "I can't believe you don't like coming here."

"Who said I don't?"

Shit.

My eyes cut to his. "I just assumed…I mean, I've never seen you around here."

"If you knew my parents, you'd understand."

"Oh, I think I got a pretty good impression of them."

He snickered. "I don't think I've ever seen anyone stand up to my dad the way you did."

I sipped my soda behind a grin. "He should've been nice to you. Then he would've gotten the sweet Andi."

He grinned. "What fun would that have been?"

I shrugged, trying not to be lured in by his killer smile. "So, has he always been like that?"

He sobered quickly, pausing, considering his words. "When business is doing well, he's everyone's best friend. When it's not, you want to steer clear of him. I spent the majority of my life steering clear of him."

My lips twisted regrettably. Not everyone was lucky enough to have parents like mine.

"You're probably not going to believe this, but growing up, I was a real screw-up. A total loose cannon. If I wasn't getting suspended for fights at school, I was being hauled in by the cops for disorderly conduct."

"Can't say I'm really surprised."

I could hear his soft snicker before he continued. "I needed *something*. A way to let off steam. To get out the anger created by my father—a man whose pockets were never as fat as his desire to be wealthy. At any cost. But the very thing I never wanted to be—the bitter, careless, angry person I loathed—was the very thing I was becoming. I hated myself. I hated my father. I hated my mother for being weak and staying with him."

I didn't know what to say, so I just sat there, listening to him shed some light on the enigma that he was.

"That's when I found football. It's what I was good at. It's what I became known for. And, like magic, all the stupid shit I'd done before was erased by my ability to throw a ball. It became my outlet. It let me shut out the rest of the world. Especially my parents."

What the hell? When he was real like that with me, when I saw a glimpse of the old Drew—or at least a real human being, I found it difficult to stay annoyed at him. "So, I take it they won't be sending out the troops looking for you?"

He shook his head. "I had myself discharged."

"You what?"

"I feel fine. I look fine." His eyes dropped to his bare chest before lifting with a devilish glint. "Besides, I was going out of my damn mind in there."

Join the club.

"Is that why you came to taunt me at therapy?" I asked.

"I wasn't taunting you. I was keeping my eyes on *him*."

I ran my finger over the evaporation on my soda bottle. "Why?"

"Because I know what he was thinking the second you walked through that door."

"I've got my work cut out for me?"

He held my gaze and shook his head. The light green flecks in his eyes were so prominent under the overcast sky. God, he was pretty. But *mean*. I needed to remind myself he was mean, and had split personalities, and I didn't need that nonsense in my life. A squawking seagull flew above us, snatching away Drew's attention. "Looks like rain."

I nodded, releasing a quiet sigh.

"There's nothing like swimming in the rain."

"Yeah. Too bad I can barely walk."

"Oh, come on. Live a little." He jumped to his feet, bending toward me.

I grabbed hold of my chair, closed my eyes, and screamed bloody murder.

Drew burst into a deep bellowing laugh. My eyes popped open. His head fell back and his shoulders shook as if his true self just burst free for all to see. As if the angry Drew had disappeared. As if he'd been holding back for far too long.

And let me just say. It was a true sight to be seen.

He dropped back into his chair and scrubbed his hands over his face. "Fuck, that felt good." He lay back, smiling and shaking his head incredulously.

"Glad I make you laugh."

"Sweetheart, you do a whole hell of a lot more than make me laugh."

His serious tone knocked my heartbeat into full gear. Or maybe it was his use of the word *sweetheart* and the slight southern drawl accompanying it. I looked back to the ocean. A couple strolled at the water's edge hand in hand. I wondered if Drew ever had a real relationship. One with sweet moments like that. Not just insignificant hook-ups with groupies.

"You annoy the hell out of me." His voice cut through, grinding my thoughts to a stop.

"Wow. You really know how to sweet talk a lady."

"Your damn persistence makes me angry as hell," he continued.

"Says the creepy stalker."

One side of his mouth lifted. "I wasn't finished...You talk more than any girl I've ever met."

"Maybe that's because you only spend time with girls like Betty."

He smiled. "You're sarcastic and feisty."

"Feisty?"

Holding my gaze, he nodded. I wondered if that was the look that made girls go home with him. The one that got them to cater to his every whim. "And you turn me on like nothing I've ever felt before."

Ummmm. Chin meet lap.

"And the thought of you with your legs wrapped around another guy keeps me awake all damn night."

My response shot out before I could even think straight. "I didn't realize you were into that sort of thing."

"Not *seeing* you with another guy. The thought of you *with* another guy. Fucking another guy. It makes my blood boil."

At that point, I'd stepped into the freaking twilight zone. My head spun and heat shot to the center of my core. "But why? You hate me."

"I don't hate you. I hate what you make me feel."

I blinked. Hard. "Well, I hate you."

He laughed sardonically. "You should. I've messed up with you. I *am* messed up. More than you could possibly know."

I shook my head. "There's no way you're any worse than what I already think."

He laughed again, this time showing his straight white teeth all the way back to his molars. In that moment, I actually felt as if I'd gotten the old Drew back. He threw his legs off the side of the chair and faced me. His eyes swept over my face, his breathing staggered. "I need to touch you."

I suddenly understood that fine line between love and hate. Because both emotions fought for control within me as I sat there lost. Lost in his words. Lost in his eyes. Lost in the alternate reality where sense and logic disappeared and I didn't even care. "I dare you."

The clouds chose that moment to open wide. Giant hard drops splattered down all around us. We both looked up and smiled as the rain showered over our faces, drenching us completely.

In one quick motion, Drew jumped up and swept me into his arms.

"What are you doing?" I linked my arms around his neck, hanging on to his wet skin for dear life.

"Oh, you know exactly what I'm doing." He charged off the patio, down the beach, and right into the ocean with me clutched to his solid chest. "You said you needed a shower."

Our laughter mixed with the melody of rain pelting the ocean's surface. I threw back my head and closed my eyes as Drew spun me around. I extended my arms and envisioned myself flying like one of the many seagulls soaring through the sky. It had been so long since I felt that free. Free of my cast. Free of the hospital. Free of my anger. Free of my ever-changing emotions.

"How do I make it so you don't forget me?"

My eyes flew open. "What?"

Drew stopped spinning. He stared down at me with clumped eyelashes and raindrops running down his flushed cheeks. Our faces lingered mere inches apart. "I want more moments like this with you."

I swallowed down my surprise, blindsided yet again by this new side of Drew.

But he didn't wait for me to respond. Instead, his lips crashed down on mine. I had no time to react before his tongue plunged inside my mouth. My hands went to his soaked hair, digging in, pulling him closer. My entire body relaxed into his kiss. The swoop of his tongue. The pressure of his lips. He knew how to kiss. He knew how to possess with the force of his lips and the depth of his tongue stroking inside my mouth. It was a dance, a race even, and I willingly followed.

What the hell am I doing?

As if he'd heard my internal indecision, he pulled back, his chest heaving in tandem with mine. The intensity of his stare set my body ablaze.

"Okay," I said breathless.

"Okay?"

I nodded. "I may be just as crazy as you, but I want more moments like this, too."

His eyes darkened—the complete opposite of what I expected. Was he angry I called him crazy? Turned off by my willingness to acquiesce? You just never knew with him.

He turned us toward the beach, trudged through the water, and up the beach.

I expected him to put me down on the patio, but he didn't. He walked us straight through the open back door and into the house, leaving huge puddles on the marble hallway in our wake.

What the hell am I doing?

He stepped inside an ocean-themed bedroom in the back of the first floor and lowered me to the bed. I expected him to follow, to hover over me, to press me into the white down-comforter, but he didn't. He stood at the foot of the bed and stared down at my drenched body. His eyes focused on my green T-shirt clinging to my chest. Given my chilled body, I must've been giving him quite a show.

He wasted no more time.

He knelt on the bed at my feet and reached for the waist of my shorts. He slipped the button through its hole, his fingertips grazing the skin on my stomach, trailing lightly to my hips. Grabbing hold of the material there, he worked my shorts down, careful of my leg and knee. Once he'd cleared my feet, he discarded them on the floor.

Laying there in my wet T-shirt and black boy-short underwear was a little unnerving…and drafty. But my entire body hummed as soon as Drew stood up and unbuttoned his shorts, letting them fall to his ankles. He shook them off and stood at the end of the bed in nothing but his black boxer briefs.

Did he want me to stare? To admire the body he'd been graced with? Or was he daring me to take off my shirt?

Game on.

I pushed myself up and grabbed the hem of my shirt, peeling the wet cotton over my head.

Oh, yeah. I've totally lost my mind.

Drew's smoldering eyes took in my nearly naked body. Thank you, Logan, for bringing my matching push-up bra. Waves of ripples rolled over me as I stared into his eyes, daring him to drop his boxers. It didn't take much coaxing. He linked his thumbs inside the elastic, right by the pronounced V chiseled into his lower abs, and pulled them to his feet.

I didn't know where to look. At his gorgeous face damp with rain totally hot for me in that moment. At his finely chiseled chest soaked and gleaming. At his manliness in all its glory.

My indecision was cut short.

Drew crawled up the bed, stalking me like helpless prey until his body covered mine. "Is this okay? Am I hurting you?"

My eyes lifted to his face, hovering inches above. Could I really go through with it? Our eyes locked for an intense moment. Uncertainty quickly transformed to want. Need. Desperation. "No." It came out a mere whisper.

That's all it took. Our lips collided. This time hungry. This time taking no prisoners. Our teeth clashed, our tongues twisted, our bodies morphed into one. My fingers tangled in his soaked hair, holding him to me. His fingers dug into the skin at my hip as he pressed himself into the already damp strip of fabric between my legs.

My head pushed deeper into the pillow as my back arched. He rocked slowly against me sending sensations pulsing everywhere. My head didn't have time to wrap itself around the fact that I was about to sleep with a guy I hated. One who, until minutes before, I was sure hated me.

The rational me wanted to pull back and ask for a minute. The reckless me wanted all of him and everything he'd willingly give.

Drew moved from my lips to the sensitive skin below my ear. His hips continued rocking in tempo with my heartbeat echoing in my ears, tempting me with all that was him and everything he had to offer. The warmth of his breath traveled over my damp skin. "God, I've wanted to do this since the second I saw you."

My eyes squeezed shut, holding back the tears prickling the backs of them. It wasn't what he said, or even the sexy voice he used to say it. It was the mention of our first meeting. But which one? Everything was so screwed up. So freaking confusing. My eyes popped open. "Tell me."

His hips kept moving as he pulled his lips away from my neck and smiled down at me. "Tell you what?"

His smile made me want to rip off my own panties and feel the true length of him between my legs. "Tell me what you remember."

"You. I remember you." He leaned down, whispering gentle kisses along my earlobe.

I was almost afraid to ask. "Where?"

"Where?" he sounded amused.

"Where?" I confirmed. I wanted to hear the truth. I couldn't be sure why. But I needed it in that moment.

"In the hospital. By my bed."

All the air left my lungs.

"I was all alone, but you were there." He pulled back to meet my gaze. "Something about you being there—your presence—it put me at ease." He lightly brushed my wet hair back from my face with his fingertips. "Like I needed you. Only you...It was like I already knew you."

My breath caught in my throat.

His eyes narrowed. "Why were you there?"

I tilted my head, taking in the confused look on his face. I completely understood his confusion. The circumstances that brought us to that moment *didn't* make any sense. And while this Drew was complex and screwed up, in that moment, he was exactly what I needed. "I felt like I already knew you, too." My hands tightened in the back of his hair. I pulled his lips down to mine, sucking his bottom lip into my mouth, teasing and nipping before moving to the top and doing the same. I needed to taste him. I needed to possess him. My tongue pushed inside his mouth. He groaned as it tangled with his.

God. I loved that sound.

Loved knowing he wanted me.

He pulled his lips from mine, burying them in my neck. He nibbled my wet skin with open-mouthed kisses, licking and sucking down my collarbone. His hand slid down the bare skin at my sides to the tops of my boy-shorts. Slipping his fingers inside, he dragged them down my legs. Somehow, without even removing his lips from my skin, he unhooked my bra and slipped that off, too.

The moment our bare bodies touched, an explosion of sensation rocked through me.

He pulled his head back. I could see it in his eyes. He felt it, too. But he said nothing. He just stared down at me as his erection pulsed between my thighs. "You sure about this?"

I shook my head.

I felt it the second my response registered because his weight lifted and he tried to roll to the side of me. I grabbed hold of his massive biceps, stopping him from leaving me. His eyes cut back to mine. "What?"

"This is going to happen," I assured him. "Us. Naked. Going at it like rabbits. But it's definitely not the best idea I've ever had."

That cocky smile I'd come to both love and despise swept across his face. "First of all, it was my idea. *And,* I plan to change your mind. Thoroughly." His lips slammed down on mine. This time greedy. This time with something to prove. This time claiming me and all I would give in that dark room with the rain bouncing off the window panes.

His hips kept a slow pace, his length gliding slowly across my wet flesh, pushing slightly without entering. He was enjoying the feel of our skin. *I* was enjoying the feel of our skin. Touching. Sliding. Invigorating.

"You feel amazing," he purred.

"Just imagine what you'll be saying in five minutes."

"You feel *fucking* amazing."

"Oh my God." I hid my face in the crook of his neck and shook with laughter. I liked this Drew. Or at least this side of him. He *could* be funny and gentle. Too bad he usually disguised it with anger. In that moment, though, his anger and other indiscretions were forgotten. I lifted my hips to meet his lazy thrusts.

It didn't take him long to figure out what I wanted. What I needed to ease the throbbing. He reached inside the nightstand and pulled out a square packet. Tearing it with his teeth, he reached down between us, his knuckles purposely grazing my wet folds and sending shivers rocking through me as he rolled on the condom. He pressed his hard flesh against my dampness. I spread my legs wider. When I did, he didn't hesitate. He thrust inside. Deep inside. And then some.

We both arched, our heads tilting back, expelling delicious, needful groans.

"*God*," I moaned. "Just like that." He was larger than I expected, so much more so than my ex. No wonder girls were lined up for him. No wonder I wasn't resisting.

At. All.

"Just like that, Drew."

"Oh, this has definitely been worth the wait," he ground out as he buried his face in my neck, assaulting me with hot, biting kisses as he pounded into me.

My fingers dug into the corded muscles in his back. So hard. So lean. So smooth. I wanted him closer. I wanted him to shield me from the outside world.

"This is not going to last long."

"Hot shot quarterback a twenty-second man. Who would've thought?"

He laughed into my neck. "Twenty now. Twenty later. I've got all night."

Twenty seconds came and went as the sheen of sweat on our bodies moved us as one. Eventually, everything I'd been holding back, everything I felt for this guy—everything I didn't want to feel for this guy—

built up into a tightly wound spool in my core. My entire body buzzed. My skin tingled. One deep thrust and I'd be there. My nails dug into his back as I urged him on. He took the hint, thrusting deep a few more times, before sending my proverbial spool unraveling at an unprecedented speed. I could barely catch my breath as my entire body quivered.

Drew followed shortly after me, dropping his forehead to mine as he gasped for breath. "We will do that again."

"I'm gonna need more than twenty seconds."

His stomach bounced with laughter off of mine. "It's you. I can't control myself."

"I have a feeling you say that to all the girls to make them overlook the fact that you've got no stamina."

"No stamina?" He dragged his teeth over his bottom lip. "I'd call that a challenge."

"Call it what you—"

Drew captured my lips, and there was nothing gentle about it. His tongue pushed inside as his erection seemed to harden inside of me. His hips started moving again. He pulled back, his eyes focused on my lips. "I love a challenge."

* * *

I woke to crisp ocean air seeping into the room. Drew's strong arms were wrapped around me. His hard chest pressed into my back, his nose buried in my hair. I didn't move. Mainly because I couldn't. But also because I loved the feel of his embrace and his fresh scent overwhelming my being.

"Morning," he murmured into my hair as his arms tightened around me.

My body relaxed at the confirmation that I wasn't some groupie he planned to toss out of his bed. At least that's what I hoped his death grip meant. Oh, and his first words hadn't been 'What the fuck?' So there was always that. "Hi."

"What are you thinking?" his raspy morning voice purred.

He couldn't see it, but I smiled. "What's the closest route to the door."

His laugh rumbled behind me, his chest bouncing off my back. "It's through the door and to the right. But you're crazy if you think you can outrun me."

I bit down on my bottom lip to stop from giggling like a teenager. "So, you are keeping me your prisoner."

"Oh no. My sex slave."

I squirmed, pretending to try to break free. Instead of tightening his hold, he loosened his arms just enough for me to twist to face him.

His playful eyes, hooded by adorable droopy lids, stared down at me. "You're not going anywhere. I'm nowhere near ready for this to be over."

How had we gone from what seemed like bitter enemies to this? I'd barely had time to wrap my head around how it happened or even if I was happy it had happened. Don't get me wrong. I'd never regret the amazing sex. The guy was freaking unbelievable with his hands. Scratch that. With every part of his body. But the whole idea that we ended up there together, in more ways than one, when we could barely tolerate each other...the jury was still out on how I really felt about that one.

"I do eventually have to get home. You may be forgetting, but I've been in a hospital since someone tried to off me."

His eyes suddenly clouded over and sadness—no, indecision—swept over his face.

"Hey. I'm fine. They messed with the wrong girl. Andi Parker doesn't go down that easily."

His eyes didn't budge from mine.

I lifted my palm to his cheek. He pressed his morning stubble into it. I imagined it rubbing against other areas and my body buzzed like a livewire. "If I didn't know any better—in other words how good I am in the sack—I'd think you're having regrets," I teased.

"What?" He shook off whatever plagued his mind, rolling on top of me and forcing me onto my back, still careful of my leg and knee. He caged me in with his arms on either side of my head. "If anyone's having regrets, it should be you."

I smiled up at him, mere inches from his lips. "Why do you think I was trying to sneak out?"

His smile matched mine. "You really are pretty amazing."

I tilted my head. "You're just figuring this out now?"

"Nope. Last night when your clothes came off, I was pretty damn sure."

Laughter rushed out of me as he leaned down and trailed kisses along the swell of my breasts. "That's all it took? I wish I knew that sooner."

"Yeah. I wouldn't have given you so much shit if you just stripped."

I shoved at him playfully. "Then why did you?"

He pulled back enough to look up at me. "I'm not an easy person to get along with."

"Shocker."

He flashed a fleeting grin. "Seriously. I know I make it tough for people to get close to me. To really let them in. But I think it's just my way of trying to keep the wrong people out."

"Did you ever consider that you might be pushing the right ones away?"

He averted his eyes for a long moment. I could tell he was considering my question. When his gaze shifted back to mine, he gave a slight shrug. "Probably. But that's why with you...from the start...I knew there was more than meets the eyes." He rolled onto his side and tore the sheets off our naked bodies, giving me the once over. "Though what meets the eye is pretty fucking unbelievable."

I looked him dead in the eyes. "I'm no Betty."

"No, you're definitely not a stripper."

My eyes widened. "So, she is?"

He shrugged. "Stranger things have happened."

"Like you and me ending up here?"

"There's nothing strange about that."

That's what you think.

As if he'd heard my thoughts and didn't like what he'd heard, he pressed me into the mattress and had his way with me again. This time he took his time. This time he made sure it lasted.

* * *

I lay there with my head on Drew's chest enjoying the sounds of the ocean waves crashing outside. And while I could've stayed like that forever, it was already early afternoon, and I needed to get home. Needed to get back to reality. "Are you taking me home or should I call a taxi?"

"What kind of dick do you think I am? I'll call the taxi."

I lifted my head so I could see his eyes. "I hate you."

"No you don't. You hate that you like me." His cocky grin slid into place. "Now get that sexy ass in the shower and leave the door unlocked."

"You're not going to carry me? I was seriously getting used to it."

"Don't be one of those needy girls. It doesn't fit you."

I scoffed. "I'm like one of the neediest girls going right now."

He rolled out of bed in all his naked glory. I wouldn't have been human if I didn't take in the beauty which was Drew's amazing body, all cut and perfect and covered in my scent.

His lips pulled up on one side. "If you keep looking at me like that, I may just need to get back in bed."

I motioned him back with my index finger.

He leaned down, pressing his palms into the mattress. I trailed my finger down the pronounced slope running down the center of his chest, hoping my touch ignited the same fire in him that his ignited in me every time he'd touched me. But instead of climbing back under the sheets, he slipped his hands under my naked body and lifted me up. "You win."

I linked my arms around his neck. "You sure this has nothing to do with stopping me from sneaking out?"

He shook his head as he walked us into the bathroom. "Not anymore." Stepping inside the shower, he lowered me gently to my feet, giving me time to get my balance before relaxing his grip on me. He flipped the knob and wrapped his arms around me, taking much of the weight off my legs as we stood under the spray of water for a long time just holding one another. Even after spending the night with him, everything about him still overwhelmed me. His towering height. His impressive strength. His irresistible presence.

"This might sound crazy," I said with a smile in my voice. "But I kind of like being your sex slave."

He flashed a grin that would have melted my panties had I not been buck naked in the shower with him. "Oh, yeah?"

I nodded.

He stepped forward, pressing my back into the cold wet tiles. He grasped my face between his hands and sealed his lips over mine. His tongue dipped inside, sweeping, stroking, devouring me whole. His knee spread my legs and his erection pressed into me, standing tall against my stomach.

I reached down and grabbed hold, running my hand up and down his solid length. He groaned into my mouth and pushed his hips into my grasp.

That just made me more eager to please him. More eager to bring him pleasure.

He pulled away from my mouth, dropping his eyes and hands to my breasts. He watched himself as he swept the pads of his thumbs over my nipples until they puckered under his touch, sending zaps of pleasure rushing between my legs and weakening my already fragile knees.

Satisfied with my responsive body, his mouth lowered down, sucking on my right nipple while his hand tugged gently on my left.

My eyes rolled into the back of my head as he alternated between the two, swirling his tongue then scraping his teeth across the hypersensitive bud.

"I can't get enough of you," Drew hummed into my chest.

His erection began to twitch in my hands. I knew he wouldn't last much longer. "I want you inside of me," I said breathlessly, my mouth overtaken by the overstimulation happening to my body.

His lips pulled back and my breast popped free from of his mouth. He stood up and dropped his forehead to mine, his fingers tugging playfully on my nipples. "You're killing me right now."

"Me?" I could barely focus with the sensations rushing through me.

"I don't have any more condoms," he grated through clenched teeth.

I worked my hand harder and faster. "I know how to improvise."

Drew growled, which quickly transformed into a groan. He pulled his hands from my body and slapped them against the wall beside my head, bracing himself. "Fuck, Andi. Fuck. Fuck. *Fuuuuck.*"

I kept my hand moving, working him through it, loving the honesty in his release. He kept his forehead to mine even after he'd finished, his breath pushing through his nose as his chest heaved. "Promise me we'll do that again."

I laughed, noncommittal. Guys said lots of things after a few good orgasms. Chances were I'd never see him again. The thought immediately silenced my laughter, tightening an unwelcome knot in the pit of my stomach.

Drew pulled back, his eyes locking on mine. "No, I'm serious. Promise me we'll do it again."

I looked up into the stormy green oceans gazing down at me. He was serious. And though I wished I didn't, I really liked that he was. "Okay."

His shoulders relaxed. "Thank God."

We spent the remainder of the shower taking turns washing each other. Once he'd finished washing my body—and I mean every inch of my body, leaving no spot ignored—I moved the sudsy loofah over his, examining every part up close for the first time. His rippled abs. His muscular back. His strong legs. The dimples above his ass. Every inch better than the last.

"I'm holding you to that promise," he said as I moved the loofah over his shoulders.

"Are you that worried you won't get laid once I'm gone?"

Deep ridges formed in his forehead.

"Girls might be scared to touch you," I explained. "Once they find out you were in a coma."

"What girls?"

I shrugged. "I don't know. Groupies. Other girls."

"I'm not interested in other girls."

My stomach fluttered, dipped, and rolled. He couldn't be serious. Though every part of me hoped he was. "Drew? You never told me what happened to you."

Darkness flashed in his expression. "You never asked."

"Well, I'm asking now." I dropped the loofah to my side. "What happened?"

He averted his gaze, speaking quickly. "I did something stupid."

My entire face scrunched up. "Playing football?"

He did one of those shrug-nods.

I could tell by his rigid body that he didn't want to talk about it. And despite how it may have seemed, I did know when not to push. "Well, you planning on doing it again?"

His eyes jumped back to mine and he shook his head. He didn't even try to conceal the seriousness in his voice. "No."

"Well good. Because I really don't feel like talking to your mute self again. Or dealing with those awful side effects."

I thought my teasing would change the tense mood created by my prying, but it remained serious as the water cascaded over us. "I don't want whatever this is to be over."

I lifted my hand to his wet cheek. "Why do you sound so serious?"

"I know we've had our issues."

"That's an understatement."

He didn't smile. "I just don't want there to be any confusion." He tried to smile, but I could see something else there. Hesitance. Fear.

Attempting to ease his mind, I nodded. "Sure. No confusion."

An hour later, he escorted me up to my second-floor condo. It felt strange being back in my building. And even stranger having him there, outside my door, staring awkwardly down at me. After everything that happened between us, I was pretty damn certain about my uncertain feelings for Drew Slater. And they weren't going anywhere, anytime soon.

He forced a smile. "You've got my number. I expect you to use it. Often."

"What happened to me annoying you?"

A sly smile spread across his lips—the same lips I'd have trouble *not* dreaming about after he left. Lips that had excelled at making my body very *very* happy. "Things change."

"Who's to say I won't get needy and text you every hour?"

He shook his head. "You won't. But just so we're clear, I'm not opposed to late night booty calls. As a matter of fact, I welcome them."

"Well, I guess you're just gonna have to wait and see."

The smile slipped from his face and he nodded. Then he leaned in and pressed his lips gently to mine, tasting them like they were something he wanted to savor. Something he'd never feel again.

Then he stepped back and was gone.

CHAPTER FOURTEEN

"Booty call?" Logan repeated, intrigued as ever with the details of my sex life.

I lifted a glass of wine to my lips, nodding from the spot beside her on my sofa.

"So? How was it?"

"Come on." I dropped my head back against the sofa cushion, unsure if I wanted her to work for it, or if I just wanted to keep the memory to myself for a little while longer.

"What? I'm your best friend. We tell each other everything. Remember when you told me about Kyle's small package?"

"Small? It was none existent."

"But you told me. And what about the funky thing Craig did every time he came? You told me that, too."

"Ugh. God. Remember that?"

"Remember? It's there with me every time I'm in bed with a guy. Hoping and praying nothing like that *ever* happens to me."

I laughed, trying to shake the horrid image from my own mind.

"Now spill it."

"Fine." I considered how to accurately capture what happened between us, doubting I could do it justice—do *him* justice. "Whatever you're thinking, it was better. *A lot* better."

Her eyes shot wide with envy. "I've had my fair share of football players. But this one's a quarterback and heading to the pros—"

"Might be heading to the pros," I corrected.

"All I'm saying is he can obviously do more with that hot body than just throw a football."

It came out before I could stop it. "Got that right."

She slammed her hand down on the armrest. "You lucky bitch."

I smiled. "Yup."

"Are you gonna call?"

I shrugged. "It's screwed up, don't you think?"

"What? Two hot people fucking. Not at all."

I tilted my head. "Us. Me and him."

"What do you mean? The fact that you hallucinated him? Did you tell him?"

"God, no. How pathetic would that sound? No, I'm talking about the fact that we hated each other."

"Hated. Past tense. Now you're getting busy."

I gnawed on my bottom lip. Was that what we were doing? I hadn't heard from him since he left hours before. Not that I expected to. But still. I wondered if out of sight for him meant out of mind. Avery said he didn't need to do more than snap his fingers and girls were there ready to oblige. Why would he be waiting for me?

"That's if you have the balls to call him," Logan challenged.

She left a little while later, giving me time to consider her none-too-subtle push to call him. Drew and I did get on well—in bed. But out? How would that even work? Prior to our time at the beach house, most of our conversations had either been arguments or ended in arguments.

I picked up my cell and scrolled through my contacts, staring down at his name on the screen. Could I do it? *Should* I do it?

A knock on my door pulled me from my phone. I maneuvered myself up from the sofa with my crutches, trying to take the weight of my boot as I moved to the door. "Who is it?"

I was greeted by silence.

I gripped the knob, reluctant to open it. Officer Roy had put me on edge, doing a real number on my already overactive imagination.

Another knocked jolted me back, speeding up my heart.

"Who is it?"

Instead of an answer there was another knock.

What the hell? "Just so you know." Yes, I was speaking to a door. "I'm not opening until I know who's there. I've seen enough movies to know there are serial killers out there who prey on girls who live alone."

"And if I were a serial killer," Drew's deep voice informed me, sending chills up my arms. "You just made a huge mistake."

I tried unsuccessfully to suppress a grin. "And what's that?" I looked down at the black yoga pants and off the shoulder top I'd been wearing since he dropped me off. *Could be worse.*

"You told me you're all alone in there. Big no-no."

I ripped the spare hair band off my wrist and quickly pulled my hair up into a messy ponytail. With a nervous smile, I grabbed the knob and pulled open the door. "Have at me, serial killer."

Drew stood with a paper bag in his arm and a grin. His baggy gray sweatpants hung low on his hips and his black Henley outlined every glorious muscle. *God*. He was so good looking I almost needed to look away.

He stepped forward. I expected him to come at me, move in for a kiss, plant his hands on my body, push me against the wall and have his way with me. But instead, he brushed right by me, causing me to shuffle to the side as he walked inside my condo like he'd been there a hundred times before. "You didn't call." He set the paper bag down on the island that separated my small kitchen from my living room.

I closed the door then turned, staring across the room at him. "It's been like eight hours."

"So, you were gonna make me wait?"

"Um…"

His eyes stayed on mine as he reached inside the bag. "How long?"

I lifted one shoulder. "I don't know."

He didn't respond right away, letting my answer stew. I wondered if he'd ever had to wait for anything in his life, especially a girl. "I hope you like Chinese food." He pulled take-out boxes from the bag and placed them on the island.

"You brought dinner?"

He turned and opened my cabinets, rummaging through until he found two dishes. "What'd you expect?"

I shrugged, surprised by how comfortable he looked in my kitchen. In my condo. In my life. "Seeing as though I had no clue you were coming by, I didn't expect anything." *Except maybe a bottle of vodka and two shot glasses.*

He eyed me across the two rooms with one of those grins that would've gotten him in my pants, had he not already have been there. "You'd make this a lot easier if you just came in here and showed me where the forks and knives are."

I laughed to myself as I maneuvered my way over to the kitchen stool. "To the left of the fridge."

He nodded, pulling the utensils from the drawer and laying them beside our dishes.

I opened the boxes, staring down at all the rice, noodles, and chicken dishes he'd brought. "Hungry?"

He slid onto the stool beside me and dug right into the noodles. "You might say I had quite a workout this morning."

I could feel the heat creeping into my cheeks. "You might say," I echoed.

He spooned the noodles into a pile in his dish. "I actually want to apologize for that."

Every muscle in my body tensed. "Apologize?"

He nodded as he dug into the rice, spooning a heaping mound into his dish. "Yeah. It never should've happened."

A knot formed in the pit of my stomach. "Oh?"

He dropped the serving spoon and turned toward me. "You're different."

"Different?" I couldn't disguise the disgust in my voice.

He placed his hands on my thighs, grasping them gently. "I should've treated you like someone I wanted to hold onto. Not someone I never wanted to see again."

My brows inverted. "What does that mean?"

He smiled. "It means, I should've taken you out. Shown you off. Treated you the way a girl like you should be treated."

"And how should a girl like me be treated?"

He looked me dead in the eyes. "Right."

The tension released from my body and the knot unfurled in my stomach. "So you want to take it slower?"

"I can't believe I'm saying this, but yeah. I want to do this right."

A smile tugged at my lips. "This has got to be the first time in the history of man that a guy actually put on the brakes."

He laughed. "Tell me about it."

"Well, just so you know, as soon as you're ready to speed things up again, I wouldn't be opposed to another shower."

A slow sexy smile slid across his lips. "Oh, sweetheart, you can count on that."

We shared a laugh, eating the rest of our meal with the same easy banter.

When he'd cleared every last bit of food from his dish, he put down his fork. "I checked my phone all day waiting for your call."

My belly dipped. Had he really just admitted that? Weren't guys supposed to play it cool? Wait a week before calling? He'd waited less than eight hours and shown up. He was breaking all the rules. And for what? Me? "Should I be flattered or worried about your stalker tendencies?"

He laughed his smooth raspy laugh. "I don't usually make a habit of caring whether I hear from a girl or not. But I told you, you're different. So I wanted you to know. I wanted you to see you affect me."

Gulp. "Well, you could've called me, too, you know?"

He dragged his fingers through his hair. All the honesty clearly unnerving him. "Yeah. Well, this is all new for me."

I put down my fork and pressed my napkin to my mouth, more to cover the smile itching to break free than to clean my lips. "What is?"

"Dating someone."

I looked into his eyes, searching for indecision or maybe dishonesty. "Is that what we're doing?"

"I hope so," he said, sporting the most vulnerable smile I'd ever seen.

To avoid turning into a big pile of mush before his eyes, I stood without my crutches and picked up our dishes, limping awkwardly to the sink.

"What are you doing?" He jumped to his feet and pulled the dishes from my hands. "I got these. Sit down."

Realizing walking on my boot wasn't the best decision, I moved slowly back to my stool. I watched as Drew placed our dishes in the dishwasher. He really did look at home in my space. But he still hadn't touched me. How slow did he plan on taking things?

He picked up the boxes from the island and moved to the refrigerator. "I watched some of your races."

My head flew back. "You did?"

He nodded while placing the boxes on my bare shelves. "There were a bunch of them online."

"Yeah. I spent so many hours watching and analyzing those races, trying to find any little thing I could do to shave seconds off my time. I haven't watched them since my accident. I haven't had the nerve."

He kept his back to me as he turned to the sink and washed his hands. "Well, for what it's worth," his voice became serious. "You were amazing."

Though he wasn't looking at me, I shrugged. "Was."

He grabbed a dish towel and dried his hands over the sink. "You'll get back there, Andi. I could see it in the way you ran. In the way you lit up at the finish lines." He finally turned to face me. "For you, it's the only option."

A silence passed between us. Was he right? Would I get back there? Was it my only option? "I didn't watch any of your games."

Creases lined his forehead. "Why would you?"

I tilted my head. "Why'd you watch mine?"

He shrugged. "Curiosity."

"You sure it wasn't to see me in my booty shorts?"

A flash of something—recollection I hoped—passed in his eyes as he grinned. "There is definitely something to be said for whoever invented booty shorts."

I snorted. "So what would I have seen if I watched you in action, besides your own tight uniform?"

He lifted a shoulder. "Not much. Just perfection."

Laughter erupted from both of us.

"Oh, I almost forgot." He walked back over to the island and reached into the paper bag he'd brought. "Dessert." He pulled out a huge bag of gummy worms.

I threw back my head and laughed. "You do know all that sugar isn't good for you, right?"

"Fuck that." He dropped down beside me. "My girl likes gummy worms. We eat gummy worms."

My girl?

He tore open the bag with his teeth. The thought of him ripping open the condom wrapper flashed in my mind and my body hummed. I watched him stuff a few worms into his mouth, letting them dangle out, before sucking them in, Andi-style. "Did I do it right?" he asked between chews.

I reached into the bag and pulled out a few. I stuffed them into my mouth, letting them dangle out. Before I could suck them in, Drew leaned over and latched onto the exposed pieces, touching his lips to mine.

My breath hitched at the unexpected heat coursing from my lips down through my veins. Was it the touch of his lips or the recollection of everything that transpired earlier? Whatever it was, it set my body on fire. There was no way we could go from rolling around naked together to whatever this was we were doing right now.

Without warning, Drew sucked the worms right out of my mouth.

That was unexpectedly hot.

He pulled back, chomping down the chewy candy. Desire clouded his ridiculously pretty eyes as they bore into mine.

Mine must've looked the same. Because if I didn't want to jump his bones before, I certainly did now. Thoughts of what I wanted him to do to me flooded my mind.

It couldn't be stopped.

I leaned toward him, pressing my lips to his. He opened slightly and I licked my way inside, loving the taste of gummy worms on his tongue. Sweet, enticing, and completely turning me on. I couldn't get close enough. If not for the damn boot, I would've climbed into his lap and never let him up. Our attraction toward one another was undeniable. We just worked. And as crazy as that seemed, every part of us fit together.

Drew pulled back, leaving me panting and needy. Why did he look so unfazed? "What do you say we watch a movie?"

"A movie?" I could hear the shock in my voice.

He nodded with a knowing smirk. "A movie."

"Is this your way of getting me on the sofa so you can get me naked?"

He laughed his carefree laugh—the one I wanted to believe he reserved only for me. "No. Tonight it means we sit on that sofa." He motioned toward it with his head. "And we watch a movie."

"Will there be cuddling?" I asked to be a smart-ass.

"Cuddling?" The notion sounded foreign to him.

I nodded. "Cuddling."

"I guess there's a first time for everything."

"Oh, well then you're in luck. I'm an amazing cuddler. One of the best around."

His pretty eyes twinkled. Or at least in my biased mind they did. "Is that so?"

I nodded.

With the bag of candy in his hand, he jumped to his feet. "Race you to the sofa?"

I looked skeptically down at my boot then back to his smirking face.

"I'll give you a head start."

"No need to pity me."

"Pity you? I wanted to look at your hot ass."

I laughed as I stood and hobbled over to the sofa. I would've liked to say I wiggled a little to give him a show, but truly, I was just trying not to fall on my face as I dropped down onto the sofa.

Drew sat down beside me, resting his arm down the length of the sofa.

"First rule in cuddling," I explained. "You must be touching."

He scooted over until the entire right side of his body pressed into my left. "Like this?" he asked, as if I'd actually taught him something he didn't know.

"Yeah. And your arm needs to be like this." I reached up and grabbed his right hand from behind me and pulled it down to rest on my bare shoulder.

His fingertips traced little circles on the side of my arm, sprouting embarrassing goose bumps everywhere. "Sounds easy enough."

"Oh, but there's more."

"You don't say?" I could hear the smile in his voice.

I slipped my left arm behind his lower back against the sofa and wrapped my right arm around his torso, burrowing my head into his solid chest and yearning to feel those dips and indentations I'd run my fingers over in the shower. "See? Now you're cuddling like a pro."

"But what if I like to lie down when I watch a movie?" In one swift motion, he pulled me on top of him and shifted so his back rested down on the sofa with me on his chest. "Much better."

I stared down into his eyes, the ones looking playfully up at me. "I think I just got played."

"I had to get you where I wanted you somehow."

"And this is where you wanted me?"

"If I'm being honest, I want you in a lot of places." His voice held that sexy rasp that did crazy things to my body. "But tonight, yes. This is where I want you." His chest lowered on a contented sigh as he squeezed me with his massive arms. "This is nice."

"You say it like you've never actually cuddled on a sofa with a girl before."

"Okay, so maybe when I was thirteen, I might've spent some time on a sofa."

"Thirteen, huh? Well, from what Avery told me, girls are lined up down the street for a shot with you now. You may be underestimating the power of a good cuddle. Just think. You bring back the retired move, and you may have them lined up around the entire block."

Drew's eyes shifted toward the television we'd yet to turn on. "You can't believe everything you hear."

"I consider your best friend a legitimate source."

His eyes moved back to mine. "Yeah, well, Avery should keep his big mouth shut."

"Worried he'll scare me away?"

He shook his head. "You went head to head with Bruce Slater and lived to talk about it. I don't think you scare that easily. At least I hope you don't." Something flashed in his eyes. That same look I'd seen earlier when he made me promise to see him again.

Damage control. "So, since this is a proper date and all, any chance you're planning to get to first base?"

Drew laughed as he grasped my cheeks between his big hands. "If you play your cards right, I may try for second." He pulled my lips down to his and showed me what a proper first date make out session in a dark living room was really like. And he definitely got to second.

* * *

Sunlight illuminated my living room when I woke the next morning. I sat up from my sofa and scrubbed my palms over my scratchy eyes. Drew was gone. I faintly recalled him slipping out from beneath me at some point during the night and whispering goodnight. I'd been too exhausted to object, having only been home from the hospital for less than twenty-four hours.

I glanced toward the kitchen, hoping there wasn't much to clean up. But it was spotless, except for a piece of paper leaned up against the bag of gummy worms on the island.

I pushed myself up and hobbled to one of the kitchen stools. I lowered myself down and picked up the paper, noticing what had to be Drew's handwriting.

Thank you for a memorable first date. I completely underestimated the power of a cuddle. I want to see you again. I'll call.

My heart pitter-pattered against my chest and there wasn't a thing I could do to stop the smile that turned up my lips.

I spent the remainder of the day in sweats and a T-shirt on my sofa. Logan had a date, so I knew I'd be staying home alone. Drew hadn't made good on his promise to call yet. I wondered if he planned to make me wait, like I did to him.

I grabbed my phone from the coffee table and scrolled through my contacts until I came to his name. I could wait it out or just call and get to talk to him like I really wanted to. It didn't have to be a game. He'd been serious when he told me he wanted to call me. He'd even shown up at my place to drive the point home. So why wait?

My thumbs tapped away at the screen. A text was safe. If he was busy, I wouldn't be interrupting him. If he wasn't, he could just call me back. **Just wanted to say thanks for last night. Dinner. Gummy worms. Cuddling. You're better than you give yourself credit for.**

I hit send.

No more than a minute passed before my phone buzzed. **Can you be ready at ten a.m.?**

* * *

The sun sat high in the clear sky as I stared out the passenger window of Drew's truck. He hadn't told me where we were headed, only that I needed to dress casually. I figured a cute pair of cutoffs and a tight white T-shirt worked.

"Here we are," he announced.

My head whipped around as he pulled into an empty high school parking lot, parking near a gate leading to a football field. "What are we doing here?"

"You'll see." He switched off the ignition and hopped out.

I pushed open my door as he grabbed a backpack and my crutches from the bed of his truck. Meeting me at the door, he held the crutches while I grasped onto them and hopped out.

I took in the vacant football field as we walked toward it. "I take it we're not here to watch a game."

"Not exactly."

"You planning on showing me some of your moves?"

"Oh, I think I could show you a move or two."

I laughed as we neared the bleachers. Instead of stopping to sit down, Drew walked out onto the track surrounding the field.

The track.

My breath hitched as I faltered, pausing before following him out onto it. The rubber beneath my feet instantly transported me back in time. To the happiness running brought me. To the freedom it gave me. To the love I had for it. To the accident that stole it all away. My eyes lowered as tears glazed my vision. "Is this why you brought me here?" My voice was shaky, nervous.

"Partly." Drew's voice became soft. "I didn't mean to upset you." He lifted my chin with his finger so he could see my eyes. "I just wanted to give you a reason to get better. I can see now it was a terrible idea."

I shook my head. "No. It just surprised me, that's all."

He nodded, his eyes averting mine for a long moment. "Come on."

I expected him to head back to his truck, to take me far away from the painful reminder that I couldn't run, but instead he walked out to the center of the football field.

I followed him onto the lush grass, my crutches sinking slightly into the soil. When I reached him, he was rummaging through his backpack. He turned and walked away from me, stopping about fifteen feet away. He turned back holding a football. "You up for a game?"

I dropped my crutches and dug my hands into my hips. "You don't think you've got a slight advantage?"

"I can't help it if I played college ball."

"College ball doesn't scare me. I'm talking about my boot. I'm not a hundred percent."

He threw back his head and laughed.

There was something about that laugh that made my lady parts quiver—and my pride kick in. "Come on, hotshot QB. Let's see what you've got."

In true quarterback fashion, Drew pulled back his ridiculous bicep and released the ball in a perfect spiral, no doubt putting less of a zing on it than he usually did. I caught it between my hands and pulled it into my chest. His smile spread wide. "I didn't realize a girl catching a football would be so hot."

"I like to think I'm hot with or without a football," I teased, equally turned on by the effortless way he handled the ball.

"Oh, you're definitely hot, sweetheart."

Unable to focus with his words swirling around my mind—not to mention stepping with a boot on my foot was no easy feat, I lobbed Drew a wobbly pass. "Why football?"

His head retracted as he reached out and caught the ball. "Why do I like it?"

I nodded.

He tossed the ball back directly into my hands so I didn't have to move to catch it. "I like the rush I get on the field knowing at least six other guys are out for my blood. I like knowing I can't be touched if my line just carries out the plays we practiced. I like the way my passes sail over the heads of the defense just out of their reach before landing in my receivers' hands."

My throw carried a little better than the last, but Drew still needed to shift to catch it.

"And as opposed to being the guy who pisses everyone off, I like being the guy who everyone needs out here to make things happen." He threw back the ball. This time it stung a little, carrying some of the residual anger stemming from his memory of the past.

I threw back the ball. "That's right. I almost forgot you're a reformed criminal," I teased.

His eyes narrowed.

Uh, oh.

Without warning, he dropped the ball and charged at me, dodging around imaginary players as he set his sights on me. If I'd been steadier on my feet, I would've back-pedaled and tried to escape, but I wasn't steady. Drew easily tackled me down onto the soft grass, settling his body between my legs and kissing me hard. When he pulled back, I could see the hunger in his eyes. "I thought girls like the bad boys?"

"We like them alright. We just know they're not good for us."

His lips lifted into that cocky grin. "Oh, I can be good for you." His voice lowered. "*Very* good." He leaned down and captured my lips, showing me just how good he could be with that tongue. And then some. When he pulled back, we were both breathless. "Why track?"

I blinked my surprise. Talk about a one-eighty. "Why not track?"

"Well, what is it that makes your life revolve around it?" He lingered a few inches above me, staring down with attentive eyes.

"I like that everything basically disappears when I run. I like the quietness in my head. My parents are following their hearts. I guess I just realized I needed to follow my own. I was good at running. And I was fast. Really fast. I knew it could take me somewhere. I never imagined the Olympics, but that ended up being my—well…was supposed to be my path."

Sadness filled Drew's eyes. If I looked closely enough at my reflection in them, mine would've looked the same. "Show me."

"Show you what?"

"What it's like." He sat us up, turning his back to me.

"What are you doing?"

He glanced over his shoulder with a grin. "Giving you a piggyback ride."

I tilted my head. "Seriously?"

"You scared?"

I shook my head. "I can walk—kind of."

"Maybe I like carrying you."

I raised a brow. "I'm not a little kid."

His eyes zoned in on my bare legs before drifting up to my T-shirt stretched tightly across my chest. "Oh, you are definitely not a little kid."

I gave him a playful shove.

"Come on." He grinned. "Hop on."

Ah, what the hell.

I slipped my arms over his shoulders, and in a single motion, he lifted me onto his back. I linked my legs around his hips the best I could with my boot on, and he slid his arms under my ass. He carried me over to the track, but instead of putting me down, he began walking around the outside lane with me still clutching to his back.

"What's it like to be out here during a race?"

I pulled in a breath. Did he seriously want to know?

"Unless you don't want to tell me," he added.

"No. It's okay."

But could I accurately put it into words? It had been a while since I allowed myself to really think about it.

"It's not just one feeling. It's everything. The wind in your face." I closed my eyes and let my head fall back, trying to replicate the gust I felt every time I pushed off the starting block. I inhaled a deep breath, yearning to smell the rubber beneath me. The sweat on my face. The landscape blooming around us. "The echo of shoes clapping off the track." I listened. The repetitive clapping in my memories had been replaced by Drew's steady footsteps as he made his way around the track so much slower than my pace during a race. "The pounding of your heartbeat in every part of your body." I concentrated on my own heart's rhythmic beat as it bounced around inside, ricocheting off Drew's back. "The need to win at all costs." I thought back to my last race and the elation I felt as I passed the leader seconds before winning the race. I opened my eyes, envisioning runners ahead of us and us gaining on them.

Drew finally spoke. "I think every athlete knows that feeling."

I rested my chin on his shoulder, enjoying the view, and his solid body beneath me, as we strolled around the remainder of the track in silence.

I couldn't believe I'd actually done it. I'd gotten back out on the track without breaking down. Without feeling sorry for myself. "Thanks for doing this."

Drew shrugged.

"I'm serious. Thanks for bringing me out here. I probably wouldn't have had the nerve to do it myself."

"Yes, you would've." Though I couldn't see his face, I could hear the certainty in his voice. "I believe in you, Andi. You'll do it. You'll get back out here. No matter what obstacles stand in your way."

I held onto him a little tighter as I released a sigh. "Maybe someday."

* * *

I lay on my sofa staring up at the swirls in the ceiling. How was it that one part of my life was a complete mess while the other was getting increasingly better with each passing day? Every moment I spent with Drew, the more I began to see who the real Drew was. He didn't need to take me to the track the previous day. No one told him to do it. But he did it because he knew it's what I needed—even when I didn't.

A knock on my door instinctively sent my heart jumping. Was it him? Had he decided to surprise me again? Did he come bearing gummy worms? Because between the two of us, I was sure we could've been a lot more creative with those things.

I sat up, using my crutches to move me to the door. "Who is it?"

I expected silence, but a voice answered. "Officer Roy."

My body tensed. *Why was he here?* I pulled open the door to find him standing there in uniform.

"Mind if I come in?"

"Of course not." I stepped back so he could enter, then closed the door behind us. I gestured toward the chair. "Have a seat."

"Thanks." He sat and waited for me to do the same.

"So what's up?" I dropped onto my sofa and let the crutches fall to the floor.

"I've got some news." His foreboding tone did nothing to ease the unexpected tension in the room.

"Okay."

"As you know, the driver of the vehicle that hit you endured some major injuries, severe enough that it took some time to even get a statement."

I nodded.

"When we finally did, his story aligned with yours."

"Was he trying to hurt me?"

He shook his head. "He said it was dark. He didn't even see the guardrail until it was too late."

My breath left me all at once. "He never saw me." I don't know why the notion hurt so badly. Maybe because it meant that my life was inconsequential. That it was almost taken without someone even knowing. Without even realizing another person was there. Another person whose life could have been ripped away.

"Since your insurance covered your medical expenses, he's insisting on paying for home care."

"What? Why?"

Officer Roy shrugged. "Guilt, I assume."

"Was he drinking? On his phone?"

He shook his head.

"Well if it was an accident, I don't want his money."

"That's up to you. I'm just passing along the message."

"Did he ask to meet me?"

"No." I could see in the way his eyes shifted away from me he was hiding something. "Said he already had."

My eyes narrowed. My heart thumped faster. "When?"

He shrugged, his eyes still guarded.

I literally had to force the words out of my mouth. "What's his name?"

He tilted his head, assessing the way I nervously squeezed my hands together. "You sure you want to know?"

When his eyes lifted to mine, I held his gaze. "I need to know."

He nodded, pausing for a long beat. "Drew Slater."

The floor dropped out from beneath my feet. Weightlessness grabbed hold of my body. And just like that, the world disappeared into darkness.

* * *

Hours had passed since Officer Roy left my condo. He thought I might lose consciousness again, so he stayed on after his shift ended to keep an eye on me. It was totally unnecessary. It had just been the shock. The hurt. The confusion.

Drew *knew*.

I couldn't be sure for how long, but he knew when it mattered.

What was I supposed to do with that? What was I supposed to do with the anger? The betrayal? The hatred consuming every part of my body?

A soft knock on my front door pulled me out of my head.

I sat up from my spot on the sofa and grabbed my phone. I'd called Logan. She was the only one who'd understand. The only one who'd help make sense of it. But she hadn't answered or called back. It was just like her to drop everything and show up regardless of the time.

I grabbed my crutches from the floor and hobbled to the door. "Logan?"

There was a long pause. "Please let me in," Drew's voice pled.

The hair on the back of my neck stood on end as a million different emotions flooded my body.

If I thought I'd been angry before, multiply that by a thousand at the sound of his voice. Scratch that. The *pain* in his voice.

Oh, hell no. Fool me once...

I grabbed the knob, pausing for a beat as I tried to calm the jitters overtaking me. Could I do it? Could I face him? Could I hear him out without breaking down *or* attacking him with my fists? I inhaled a deep breath and yanked open the door. "What?"

Drew's head lowered, like he couldn't even face me.

"What could be so important that you came all the way over here to see me? What do you need to say *now*, that you haven't said every time we've been alone together?"

He glanced up from under his thick lashes. "Can I come in?"

I expelled a deep breath, resisting the urge to lash out at him. I didn't want to see him. Didn't want to hear his excuses. Didn't want to be conflicted as to how I should feel. But when he moved to step forward, I knew I could either stand my ground and block his entrance or hear him out. Being the last time we'd speak, I knew for my own well-being, for my own sanity, I needed closure.

I stepped back.

Drew brushed carefully by me, his eyes moving around my living room before settling on the chair beside the sofa. He sat down in it, leaving the sofa for me.

I begrudgingly moved to it, thankful for the distance. I leaned back and crossed my arms, preparing myself for the words that would inevitably crush me even more than I'd already been crushed. How much was I expected to endure? And how long before I totally lost my mind? Again?

Drew leaned forward, his elbows digging into his knees and his hands wringing together. It took some time, but his eyes finally lifted to mine. If I wasn't so angry—hurt, blind-sided, I might've cared about the pain etched in them and the dark circles surrounding them. "I'm sorry."

My head shrunk back. "Sorry?" It was as if that one word set off an eruption of rage. "For treating me like shit? Destroying my dreams? Hiding the truth? Which one is it? Because I'm a little confused."

He winced at the harshness in my voice. "Stop it."

"Stop what? Trying to understand this insanity?"

"This isn't what I wanted. This isn't how I wanted this to happen."

"Then tell me. How did you see this playing out? You'd tell me you're the person who stripped me of everything I cared about, and I'd say, 'No problem. It happens'?"

That anger I'd become accustomed to in the hospital clouded his guilty eyes. "I wanted to tell you. Every time I saw you. Every time I was around you. Every time you smiled. Every time you laughed. I. Wanted. To. Tell. You."

"I guess I'm glad you waited until after you fucked me. Would've seriously ruined the moment."

He jumped to his feet. "I never should have come here."

"You're right. You shouldn't have. You should have told me the truth weeks ago. But you were a coward!"

He clenched the sides of his head and roared through gritted teeth, "Fuuuuck."

There was the Drew I'd come to know. There was the angry shell of a man. Of course he couldn't stay hidden forever. "I didn't do this. *You* did this." My voice cracked and my eyes glazed with tears. "And to think. You had the balls to treat me like *I'd* done something wrong. What kind of person does that?"

He tunneled his fingers through his hair. "I never wanted to hurt you."

"A lot of good that does me now."

He stared at me across the room as my chest rose and fell, my nerves on fire. I needed this. I needed to fight with him. I needed him to hear the pain I was feeling. I needed to hurt him like he hurt me.

But even still, in that moment, he held the power to say so many things. Things that could ease the intolerable pain I was feeling. Things that could cut through the huge divide that once again existed between us. Things that could make this less screwed up. But, coward that he was, he grabbed the door knob and walked out.

CHAPTER FIFTEEN

Logan and I, along with an empty bottle of rum, sat at my kitchen island gluing bling to the top of my powder blue graduation cap. She'd convinced me once the sun hit it during the ceremony, I'd sparkle like crazy—which somehow would make me feel better. But since half a bottle of rum hadn't done the trick, I wasn't banking on it.

"Do you wish you let him explain?" she asked, treading lightly since she knew the subject was off limits.

"There was nothing to explain." I hated slurring. But with the amount of rum in my system, it was unavoidable.

"But, Andi—"

"No." My voice rose. "He did it, Logan. He hurt me. And he knew and kept it from me." I didn't mean to take it out on her, but what was I supposed to do? I wasn't dealing with it. Since Drew left my condo a week ago, I hadn't seen or heard from him. After everything I'd learned, everything I'd been through because of him, I needed to let him go. Let the notion of us go. And I was trying.

Logan's regretful expression told me she didn't know what to say. That in itself was a freaking miracle since the girl was never at a loss for words.

A knock on the front door pulled our drunken attention away from the uncomfortable conversation and my over-accessorized cap.

"Do you think it's him?" she whispered.

I wondered for a split-second if she might've been right. "No. He'd never show up here again."

She jumped to her feet. "Let me get it."

I shook her off, grabbing my crutches and moving to the door. When I reached it, I paused. "Who is it?" My heart stopped for a long torturous moment.

"Avery."

My entire body deflated more than I cared to admit.

"Who is it?" Logan whispered from the kitchen.

"Drew's friend." I grabbed hold of the knob and pulled the door open.

Avery stood alone in the hallway with his hands in his back pockets and a guilty look on his face—like *he'd* been the one who'd done something wrong.

"Luke?" Logan's voice called from behind me.

Avery's eyes flashed over my shoulder. My head did the same. "Logan. This is Avery."

Her eyes narrowed and voice lowered. "I know who it is."

I glanced to Avery whose eyes too had narrowed.

"She thinks I look like Luke Bryan," he explained. "You know. The country singer. She knows I don't like it but calls me it anyway."

"Add that to the list of things he doesn't like," Logan growled.

My eyes jumped between them, before settling on Avery. "What are you doing here?"

He tore his eyes away from Logan. "Drew said it was useless, but I wanted to come by to check on you."

"Wow," Logan nearly shouted. "It's nice to know good ol' Luke cares about *someone's* feelings."

"Avery." The poor guy sounded exasperated. "It's Avery."

My head spun toward Logan. "He's here to see *me*. So take your hurt feelings—or whatever this is going on here—and go in my room until we're done."

Her eyes went round and her jaw dropped. "Did you just put me in my place?"

"Damn right I did."

She clapped her hands as she stood a little wobbly from my kitchen stool. "It's about time my girl reappeared." She gave Avery one last glare before disappearing down the hallway.

I turned back. His eyes remained on the empty hallway. When my bedroom door slammed shut, rattling the entire condo, his eyes darted back to me.

I jabbed my thumb over my shoulder. "You want to talk about that?"

"There's nothing to talk about." He played it off like it wasn't a big deal, but his eyes betrayed him. "Can I come in?"

I shifted aside and he stepped inside, his eyes assessing my small condo. Instead of sitting in the living room chair or on the sofa, Avery kept his hands in his pockets and strolled over to the stool Logan vacated, leaning his tall body against it. "He's sorry."

I closed the door and made my way over to my sofa, resting myself against the armrest unsure if I was ready to hear him out.

"I've never heard him apologize for anything he's ever done. And some of those things have been really messed up. But now he's acting like a damn chick. He's not eating or sleeping. And if you know Drew, you know that's unheard of."

"Do you really expect me to care?"

"He's miserable, Andi."

"*He's* miserable?" My voice dripped with sarcasm.

His shoulders dropped on an exhale. "Look, I know you were hurt badly. But he can't do anything about that now. What he can do is try to make amends, but he thinks you never want to see him again."

I crossed my arms. "That's a fair assessment."

"I don't believe you."

My eyebrows inverted. "Which part?"

"I know you care about him."

"Cared about him. *Cared.* And not even that much."

"Well, just so you know, this hasn't been easy on him."

I felt my cheeks heating with anger. "I'm the one who lost everything."

He looked around my living room, his eyes stopping on the mantle over the fireplace. Pictures of me with my parents and with Logan filled the small space. "You haven't lost everything. You lost one thing. And from what I've heard, you might be able to get that back with some hard work."

"Please don't try to minimize it."

He shook his head. "Believe me. I'm not. I just know that it would crush Drew even more if you gave up on your dream because of a setback. One he had everything to do with."

I scrubbed my hands over my face, feeling mentally and emotionally drained from the unexpected lecture. "What are you a therapist now?"

He shook his head as he stood from the stool and made his way to the door. "Nope. Just someone who cares about his friend and wants to see him happy for once in his life."

With that, he walked out of my condo leaving me to ponder his words. Not to mention, even more confused than I'd been before.

CHAPTER SIXTEEN

I'd spent hours perfecting the loose curls that hung over my shoulders. Too bad all the make-up in the world couldn't conceal the dark circles under my eyes— or the scratch on my cheek. And while it was faint, I knew it was there. Just like I knew the true cause of it.

I reached up and set my bling-covered cap on my head, taking a deep cleansing breath.

My phone buzzed on my dresser. I grabbed for it, my stomach instantly dipping with excitement. "Hi."

"Sweetheart, is that you?"

A smile overtook my face. "Yeah, Mom, it's me." Tears filled my eyes as the hole in my heart shrunk slightly. I missed the sound of her voice. Hell, I missed *her*. "Are you guys okay?"

"Of course we are. It's been so difficult to get reception out here. Tell me how you're feeling?"

"Getting better every day," I lied.

"That's wonderful. It feels like we haven't spoken in months."

I wanted to say, "One month." But why waste time feeling sorry for myself when I had limited time to talk to her. "I know. I tried calling you."

"What's that, sweetie? You're breaking up."

"I said I tried calling you."

"Well, we just called to say how very proud of you we are. We wish we could be there to see you walk across the stage. Good luck today. We love y—"

"I love you, too," I said, though I knew our connection had been lost.

I tossed my phone down, feeling more alone than I had in a long time. Was this what destiny had in store for me? A long road of loneliness and disappointments?

A knock on my front door carried me into the living room. "Who is it?"

There was no response.

My heart leapt to my throat. "Who is it?"

Still nothing.

I grasped the knob with a nervous grip and pulled the door open a crack. "Oh. My. God."

My parents pushed their way inside. I practically collapsed into their arms, holding onto them like I'd never let them go. "You came."

They laughed as we stood in a group hug in the middle of my living room.

"We came," my mother assured me, her beloved Patchouli oil invading my nostrils. It was so her. *And she was here.* Birkenstocks and all.

"We wouldn't have missed it for the world," my dad added. "Our baby's graduating college."

* * *

Logan met my parents and me on the quad well before any of the other soon-to-be-graduates so we could check out the seating arrangement, and determine my best route to the stage.

My head twisted around from where I sat in a borrowed wheelchair. Sure, I could've used my crutches, but it would've taken me forever to maneuver the entire way, creating a major backup of frustrated graduates.

Thousands would soon occupy the rows of seats configured in a massive U-shape filling the grassy area. Aisles ran on both sides with one down the center. The stage sat bedecked with potted plants, a podium with the UNC emblem on the front, chairs for faculty and honored guests, and piles of diplomas atop tables with black linen tablecloths.

A small set of steps sat at the side of the stage, but the ramp I'd use sat behind it. So while the other graduates made their way down the center aisle to the steps amidst excited family and friends, I'd be behind the stage, rolling out when my name was announced. Logan had offered to push me, but I'd turned her down, needing to prove I could do it.

An hour—and a bunch of pictures with my parents and Logan—later, I sat at the end of my row. The afternoon sun beat down, causing the polyester gown to adhere to my sweaty skin in all the wrong places. Having been my first all-day outing since being discharged, I could feel my energy fading quickly.

On stage, the dean droned on about perseverance and the guest speaker recounted his rise to the top of a computer software company. *Very* inspirational.

I just needed to cross that stage and be done with it all.

When the time came, everyone in my row rose to their feet. They filed to the right into the center aisle, en route to the steps at the side of the stage. I filed into the left aisle and wheeled around the back of the stage and up the ramp. I took a spot behind the small decorative curtain at the side of the stage and waited to hear my name called.

From that vantage point, I had a perfect view of the sea of blue graduates and their family members and friends baking under the scorching sun. I could see my parents and Logan eagerly waiting with their phones out, ready to capture me crossing the stage.

"Hi."

My entire body jolted and the hair on the back of my neck stood on end at the sound of the deep voice behind me.

"We're almost up."

My blond curls whipped over my shoulders. I gazed up at the dark green eyes that plagued both my dreams and nightmares for the last week. Drew wore a navy suit with the top button of his crisp white shirt unbuttoned. His hands grasped my chair's handles. "What are you doing here?"

He cocked his head. "You didn't think I'd let you do this alone, did you?"

My insides twisted. What was going on? And how could I feel excitement and disgust at the same time?

"Andi Parker," a voice on stage announced, snapping me back to the present.

"That's us," Drew said, pushing me out from behind the curtain and across the front of the stage.

I accepted my diploma from Dean Edwards, shaking his hand with a strained smile while Logan screamed my name from the center of the crowd, her voice carrying far and wide. I shot her a quick wave, having no idea where I'd be without her. I caught a glimpse of my parents looking so incredibly proud before Drew pushed me to the rear of the stage and down the ramp.

He stopped on the path behind the stage, and walked around to face me. "Congratulations." He forced a smile, then dropped to his knees, evening our eyes. "You look beautiful."

My eyes flashed away. He was not allowed to show up and do this to me. Not here. Not now.

"You deserve every good thing that comes your way."

I nodded, still finding it difficult to meet the gaze of the person who hurt me so badly. "Thanks."

With that, he stood and looked down at me for a long moment. He wanted to say something. I could see it in the tension around his eyes. It was me who wasn't sure if I wanted to hear him out, or if I just wanted him to leave. I was so confused by my feelings for him. By my unwillingness to forgive him. By my need for him.

"Andi?" my mother called.

My head whipped around. It felt strange smiling at that moment, when Drew had sent my head into such a tailspin. But seeing my parents and Logan approaching—the three people who loved me most in the world—it put things into perspective.

When I looked back to Drew, he'd already walked away as if he hadn't just shown up for the sole purpose of walking me across the stage.

Why had he? And why was my freaking heart racing?

I wiped beads of sweat from my forehead as my dad leaned down and hugged me. "Congratulations, honey." I watched Drew's retreating form over my dad's shoulder getting further and further away. "We're so proud of you."

My dad stepped back, and my mom took his place, hugging me fiercely and blocking my view of Drew entirely. "Congratulations."

"Thanks."

When she pulled back, her eyes drifted to where Drew had disappeared. "Any chance you're gonna tell me who that was?"

Logan didn't let me speak. She leaned down and captured me in a bear hug. "What the hell was that?" she whispered.

"I don't know," I murmured into her shoulder.

"Tell me you know Duke's graduating right now. Tell me you know he skipped his graduation for you."

I closed my eyes and let the notion settle. Who was I kidding? No way in hell that notion would ever settle. Why had he done it?

My parents took Logan and me to my favorite Italian restaurant by the coast to celebrate. Too bad they were the ones doing most of the celebrating, downing bottles of wine while entertaining Logan with stories of their recent adventures—which she totally loved.

I tried to don a happy face and drink enough wine to numb the pain and confusion caused by Drew's unexpected appearance, but nothing worked.

Halfway through the meal, I slipped away to the restroom and pulled out my phone. I knew what needed to be done. If I had any chance of getting over it—of moving on—I just needed to do it. I stared down at the blank screen for a long time before I finally typed out a text. **I wish it didn't hurt so much to be around you.**

I waited, staring down at my unanswered message, wondering if he'd even bother to respond. Seconds later, a text came back. **It hurts me more knowing you hate me.**

Before I'd let myself feel sorry for him, my fingers went to work. **I don't hate you. I just don't think I can forgive you.** I waited, this time with my heart pounding.

I know.

I dropped my head.

Why did everything with him have to be so freaking hard?

CHAPTER SEVENTEEN

I'd spent the week since graduation either at physical therapy or parked on my sofa watching mindless television. My parents had returned to their quest to save whales, and it wasn't like I could go anywhere easily with my driving foot in a boot. It took all my effort getting to therapy, since I obviously rejected Drew's offer for homecare. And while I knew I could go out with Logan's help, I wasn't all that fun to be around.

I flipped through the television stations looking for something to help me fall asleep—something I'd been struggling with. *Go figure.* I'd avoided ESPN for fear of talk of the Olympics, but tonight it wasn't the Olympics that had my eyes glued to the screen.

"The nineteenth pick in this year's draft is Troy Winters," the man on television announced.

The draft.

I wondered if Drew had already been selected. Or, if he'd withdrawn like he'd wanted to. Come to think of it, maybe this Drew never even considered entering the draft. It wasn't like I'd know. I'd barely gotten to know him.

I closed my eyes, trying to stop my mind from caring about the draft. Caring about Drew's future. Caring about Drew period. Maybe I was just curious since he was someone I knew. Someone I shared experiences with. Someone I…

My eyes snapped open.

That was it.

I grabbed my phone. I needed to be out of my condo. Away from the four walls closing in on me. Away from the reminder of Drew showing up at my graduation. Away from the constant ache in my chest. It. Was. All. Too. Much.

* * *

"Miss? You sure about this?" the taxi driver asked from the front seat, hesitant to leave me where I'd requested. He thought I was nuts, just like Logan when I told her where I was headed.

I handed him my cash over the seat. "I'll call you when I'm done." I scooted over and pushed open the door. With only a few feet to go to reach the guardrail, I hopped to it, careful of my booted foot.

Was I crazy?

Of course.

That had been established weeks ago.

Darkness surrounded me as I sat down on the dented metal. With my feet on the road, I twisted toward the ocean. The coastal breeze whipped my hair around as the waves crashed on the shore, violent and destructive, much like my mind.

I thought back to all the choices I'd made. All the decisions that got me to this place. All the what-ifs. What if I hadn't gone running that night? What if I hadn't ended up on this stretch of road? What if I'd joined my parents in Antarctica? What if I got to race? What if I lost and didn't make it to the Olympics after all?

"Take a walk with me."

My entire body lurched forward as my head flew around. Drew stood with his hands buried in the pockets of his jeans, his head lowered. My eyes jumped around. "Where the *hell* did you come from? Did you follow me?"

He shook his head.

I stared at him for a long time. Could I believe him? It wasn't like he'd been truthful with me in the past. How else would he have known where I— "Logan told you I was here?"

He shook his head again. "Logan told Avery and he told me."

I rolled my eyes. "Well, at least we got them talking."

"Not really. She texted him," he explained.

"Figures." I huffed out a breath as I looked out at the deserted road, bending and disappearing into the darkness as it had the night of the accident.

"Will you walk with me?" he asked again.

"I'm still not walking on my own."

His eyes jumped to the space beside me. "Where are your crutches?"

"At home."

He shook his head, clearly dismayed by my decision. Without warning he moved closer, scooping me up like a bride on her wedding night.

I yelped. "For the love of God."

"I thought you like it when I carry you?"

I threw my arms around his neck for support. "*Liked.*" I tried not to think about the last time he carried me that way. But being naked and headed for the shower was kind of tough to forget—no matter how much I wanted to.

Ugh.

Drew inched his way along the guardrail for a few more yards until we reached an opening and a set of weathered wooden steps. He took them one at a time, carefully bringing us down to the beach. I figured he'd have difficulty once we reached the sand, but he tread just as easily with me in his arms as he had the last time he carried me on the beach.

My brain searched unsuccessfully for something to say as it worked to process what was transpiring. Was I angry? Flabbergasted? Happy? "Please put me down."

"In a minute." His eyes focused straight ahead on the closest lifeguard chair.

"Oh no way in hell are you getting me up there."

He gave me the look. The one with the lifted brow that warned not to challenge him. We reached the base of the chair. His eyes drifted up it. "Hang on."

I closed my eyes and tightened my grip around his neck. I wished I didn't feel so safe in his strong arms. The ones responsible for so much pain. The ones that should've been slipping on a football jersey for the entire world to see. They extended as he gripped the steps, cautiously climbing to the top. He pivoted, then slid me smoothly onto the seat.

I opened my eyes, relieved to have made it in one piece. I focused on the dark ocean, so fierce and powerful under the light of the full moon. Though it was difficult to remain focused with Drew so close and his hip pressed against mine, I kept my eyes locked on the tide and the ebb and flow of the waves slapping upon the shore in even successions. "Any idea how you're getting me down?"

"Nope."

"That's reassuring." My mind whirled, wondering how long I could feasibly sit up there and say nothing now that I was pretty much stranded with him.

A long time passed as we sat lost in the power of the ocean. The unyielding roar of the waves. The overpowering brininess in the air seeping into our pores. The peacefulness of it all.

"I never thought I'd come back here," Drew admitted, snapping me back to reality.

"Me neither."

His head turned toward me. "Then why are you here?"

I lifted my shoulders then let them drop. Hell of a question.

"Can I tell you why I am?"

I could sense his eyes boring into the side of my face. But honestly, I wasn't sure I wanted to hear the truth. It held the power to gut me more than I'd already been gutted. I latched onto the waves, refusing to look at him, no matter what he said.

"You," he explained. "I'm here for you. Because you deserve the truth. And you deserve someone willing to give you the truth, no matter the repercussions."

Of course he had to go and say that.

"I told you I was a screw-up and that football became my outlet. But what I didn't tell you was my outlet became my biggest nightmare. People wanted to know me. Wanted to be around me. Wanted my fame—or whatever it was—to rub off on them."

I could feel him shaking his head incredulously.

"Who knows? They probably never even liked me."

The smartass in me itched to say something, but my anger and hurt superseded it.

"The better I got, the more recognition I got. Which meant the more recognition my parents got. It's what got them connected with their business partners and subsequently made them their millions. And they fucking loved it. It's what they always wanted. The money. The attention. The notoriety of being Drew Slater's parents." He laughed a humorless laugh. "But the crazy thing is, I don't think they ever really loved me."

I would not feel sorry for him. I would not.

"Football was no longer something I loved doing, it became something I needed to do for everyone else. It no longer kept out the demons. It brought them out of the woodwork. The night of the accident, I felt like I had no choice. I was going into the draft no matter what I wanted. My parents' business was failing. They were relying on *me* to get the big paycheck. My hometown was relying on *me* to put it in the spotlight. Some of my friends even planned their futures around following *me* all over the country." His grip tightened on the edge of the seat. "I know it sounds selfish, but I didn't want everyone relying on me. I wanted to get my degree, move to a small town where no one knew me, and start a new life. But everyone was making that impossible. So. Damn. Impossible. I couldn't think straight. I couldn't focus anymore."

I finally turned to look at him. His eyes were locked on the ocean as he lifted his hands and tunneled his fingers through his dark hair.

"That night, I just needed to breathe. I drove for miles—hundreds of miles—all the way from Duke. And in that split second when I saw the guardrail in front of me, I saw a way out. I don't know if I planned to end it or just hurt myself enough to be out of the draft, but I closed my eyes and floored it."

A giant gasp stole my breath.

He turned to me, his eyes ferociously honest. "I never saw you, Andi. I swear. I knew I hit something other than the guardrail, but God, I couldn't have known it was you. I *didn't* know it was you."

The air punched out of my lungs at the realization that he'd purposely caused the accident. He'd purposely hurt himself. He'd purposely hurt *me*.

God dammit.

I needed to go. I needed to climb down on my own and run far away. But I was trapped. Trapped next to the one person I needed to be away from. I turned back to the shore wishing I could un-hear what I'd heard. Wishing I could erase the past. Wishing the circumstances that brought us together could've been innocent. Not *this*. Not this screwed up drama that proved too insane to even make up.

"I don't know what else to say." His voice was pained, desperate even.

I paused for a long moment, knowing there was nothing he could say. Nothing he could do. The damage had been done. "Thank you for being honest with me." They were my words, but I had no idea how I even managed to get them out of my mouth. My pain was real. It was raw.

He nodded, but his face became tortured, making me wonder if he'd expected more. Expected me to forgive him. Expected me to forget. "Tell me how I make this better. Tell me what I need to do. Tell me how I don't lose you."

I swallowed around the boulder-sized knot in my throat, knowing there was nothing he could do—nothing anyone could do—to make it better.

Before I could say anything, words shot out of his mouth. "I miss you."

I closed my eyes, trying to shield myself from the pain in his voice. The desperation in his words. The indecision swirling inside of me.

"And I know I hurt you—God, I *know* I fucking hurt you. And I'm sorry. I'm *so* damn sorry. But I promise you, it'll never happen again."

My anxiety kicked in. If ever I were going to have a panic attack, this was the time.

"I'm staying this summer," he continued. "I want to be nearby if you need me. You can rely on me. I'll prove it to you. And then maybe, just maybe, if you ever forgive me, I'll be here."

Shock waves washed over me. "Drew—" I wasn't sure if it was a plea for him to stop or just my own pain laced with confusion.

He shook his head. "Don't say anything right now. Just know I'm here for you. *Only* you."

My head swam, totally unequipped to deal with what was happening. The bass drum pounding methodically in my chest told me I wasn't okay. None of it was okay.

The roar of the ocean enveloped us as we remained in that chair for a long time. Silent. In our own heads.

Could I forgive him? Could I overlook the pain he'd caused me? Could I forget the dreams he'd taken from me?

If it were Logan, I'd tell her to quit whining and get over it. But it wasn't Logan. It was me. How the hell was I supposed to get over it when I couldn't even wrap my head around the madness? I'd been through hell, *God dammit*, and still couldn't walk—forget about run. *That* entitled me for as long as it took.

Maybe if it had been a true accident—an awful twist of fate—I would've been able to get over it. I would've been able to let it go. But he did it purposely. And then didn't tell me.

Gahhhhh.

I held so much bitterness inside of me. I felt such resentment toward him. If I didn't know any better, I'd think I'd explode from the weight of it.

I'd never get over it. I knew myself.

I stared up at the moon, so full and bright like a spotlight above us. Too bad our story was a tragedy, not some lighthearted comedy with a happy ending that caused audience's to cheer as we took our final bow. "You got your wish."

His eyes cut to mine.

"You missed the draft."

He nodded.

"That's good."

"Yeah." The happiness he should've displayed—the relief of avoiding the draft and an unwanted fate—remained buried beneath his pain. His guilt. His knowledge that his rash decision affected someone else's fate.

"How'd your parents take it?"

"I'm staying alone at the beach house, so…" He shrugged as though that said it all. He'd known the risk of going against their wishes. I was surprised they even let him stay there—if they knew he was there.

I rubbed my hands up and down my bare arms, trying to warm them as the chilly night air quickly crept in.

"Come on. It's cold out here," Drew said. "Let me get you home."

I shook off the offer. "I'll call a taxi."

He studied my face. "Seriously?"

"How do you think I got here?"

He shook his head. "You're coming with me."

* * *

I stared out the passenger window of Drew's truck at the streets surrounding my neighborhood. I wanted to ask him if this was "the truck" or if it was a rental. But the thought of drudging up more pain seemed useless. I glanced to Drew's face, lit only by the headlights of passing cars. Neither of us uttered a single word. Because, really? What more was there to say?

When he pulled to a stop outside my building, I grabbed hold of the door handle, hoping for a quick escape. But Drew had already hopped out and circled the front of his truck, meeting me at my open door. He offered his shoulder, letting me rest my weight on him. I was surprised he didn't try to carry me again. Maybe he wanted to show me he believed in me. Believed I was strong enough to take care of myself. Regardless, he walked me to the front door. Once I'd opened it, he released his hold.

Strange thoughts invade your mind when you sever ties with someone. Thoughts of the past. Of your decision to end it. Of the future that would never be.

I stared down at the pavement, finding it difficult to meet his gaze.

Drew took a step back. "Just know, I meant every word I said."

My eyes lifted as I nodded, believing him wholeheartedly. Unfortunately, that didn't change the cold hard truth.

Without another word, he turned and headed back to his truck.

I limped my way inside the building, failing miserably at looking confident and in control. When I reached the elevator, I let out the deep breath I'd been holding and forced myself not to look back.

CHAPTER EIGHTEEN

A week had passed since that night on the beach. Drew hadn't tried to contact me. I assumed that was him leaving the ball in my court. But the longer time passed and we didn't speak, the easier it became to forget about him. Not the pain he created. What had been growing between us. I needed to hate him. I needed to hold onto that anger. I needed to hold him responsible. Because if I didn't, what did I have left?

I hobbled down to the front of my building, knowing my taxi would be arriving to whisk me off to physical therapy. My leg felt stronger. I could walk solely on the boot and no longer required crutches. Stepping out onto the sidewalk, I glanced to the right. A small girl walked a cute little dachshund. To the left—

"Hey," Drew greeted me, leaned up against my building in a ball cap pulled down low.

Ummm. "What are you doing here?" And in a hat? Did he know it was my weakness?

"Just making sure you got to physical therapy on time."

I stared at him skeptically, wondering if he'd followed me to learn my schedule. Then it hit me. "Logan?"

He shrugged, unable to hide the guilt written all over his face.

"I'm going to kill her," I grumbled under my breath, knowing full well he could hear me. "Well, thanks anyway, but the taxi's on its way."

He pushed off the building, taking one step closer then another. Soon he stood right in front of me until all I could do was look up into his eyes. "How's the leg feeling today?"

His nearness unnerved me. As did the pull his body had on mine. "Getting stronger." My taxi pulled up to the sidewalk. *Thank God.* "This is me."

He nodded. "I'm around every day. I'd be happy to drive you."

I shook my head. "I've got it covered."

I shuffled forward, but he purposely blocked my way. "I probably should've said, 'I'm around every day, and I *want* to drive you.'" The seriousness—make that determination—in his voice and the sincerity in his eyes floored me.

Flutters invaded my belly. Traitorous, unruly flutters. "Um."

He stepped out of my way. "I'll take 'um.'"

"No, I didn't…I just…can I let you know?"

He nodded, like it was more than he expected me to say. "Absolutely."

My lips shifted into a sad smile. "See ya." I opened the door and slid into the backseat of the taxi with my heartbeat pounding in my head.

Drew didn't move, just watched until the driver pulled away.

What the hell was that?

* * *

The following day, I stepped outside my building, half-expecting Drew to be waiting. If I was being honest, it's why I put on makeup for therapy and made it outside early.

I know. Stupid.

But it didn't matter. He wasn't there.

Foolishly, a part of me believed he planned to fight for me. Planned to do whatever it took, like he claimed he would. Deep down I think I always knew he wasn't that guy. He was used to girls throwing themselves at him. Why would he want someone he'd have to convince to like him? Trust him? Want him?

My taxi arrived at the rehab facility with plenty of time to spare. I made my way inside, taking a seat in the waiting room. Magazines littered the table in front of me. Of course I chose the one with the male model with the killer abs on the cover. I buried my nose in the pages for the next few minutes. I must've been overly focused on the pictures of him drenched from a workout because I never heard the door open or anyone enter the waiting room. But someone clearly sat in the chair beside me. I recognized his fresh scent and could feel his presence.

"You left without me."

My eyes lifted to find Drew's trained on mine from the seat beside me. "Just so you know, this creepy stalker thing you've got going on is starting to really freak me out."

Though I was completely serious, he laughed. "I went to your place. You weren't there."

"*See.* Creepy stalker."

"Were you avoiding me?"

My eyes averted his as I closed the magazine and dropped it onto the table. "How could I avoid you if I didn't know you were coming by?"

"I told you I wanted to take you."

I looked back at him, annoyed by his presence and put off by his presumptuous remark. "And I told you I'd let you know."

"So?"

"So what?"

"Are you going to let me know?"

The door swung open and my therapist greeted me with a smile. Her eyes instantly slipped to Drew. I saw the moment his insane good looks and overwhelming presence registered because her eyes expanded.

Ignoring her reaction—or at least trying to, I stood and made my way over to the open door behind her.

"See you later, Andi," Drew called.

I didn't bother turning around. I just disappeared behind the door, convinced more than ever that forgiving him and having any sort of relationship with him would never work. We weren't even *in* a relationship, and his persistence—and the attention he received from every female around—was already making me nuts.

After a long session of avoiding questions about Drew, I sat on the stationary bike wiping down my face with a towel.

"You're making great strides, Andi. I've never seen someone so determined to get back on her feet."

"I told you. I plan to do whatever it takes."

My therapist nodded. "It shows."

I hopped carefully off the bike. "I'll see you tomorrow."

When I stepped out into the waiting room, my head retracted.

"Ready to go?" Drew sprang up from his chair and walked over to the front door, opening it and stepping back to give me room to pass. "How'd it go in there?"

I made my way outside. *Would it be too childish to turn down his offer and call a taxi?* I hadn't actually expected him to stay and wait. "I'm pretty sore."

"That's to be expected. A long hot bath will help." He held up his palm. "Wait here. I'll get my truck."

I nodded, needing the moment to digest what was happening—what I was letting happen.

Seconds later, Drew pulled up to the sidewalk in his silver truck and jumped out. He circled the front and opened the door for me. We drove in silence for a few miles. Sure, he'd cleared his throat and coughed a couple times, but he hadn't attempted to make small talk.

Since it had been his brilliant idea to show up at therapy, I sat back and closed my eyes. I couldn't wait to take a shower. I was drenched in sweat, and my back and thighs stuck unattractively to the leather seat. I subtly dropped my nose to my shoulder, wondering if my deodorant had withstood the intense workout.

Drew peeked over and snickered. "You don't smell."

"I don't believe you."

His eyes jumped between the road and me. "First of all, I will never lie to you. Second, you've clearly never been in a locker room with fifty guys."

"A girl could only dream."

His brows pinched. "Fifty *sweaty* guys."

I scrunched my nose and shook my head.

"Well, once you have, talk to me about smelling. You smell like you always do."

"So I smell all the time?"

He laughed. "No. You smell like lavender."

I looked out the window, expelling a small sigh. Why did he have to pay attention to things like that?

"But just so you know, I'd totally be up for giving you a sponge bath."

My head whipped to him. "Why'd you say that?"

"Say what?"

"The sponge bath thing?"

A cocky smirk slipped into place. "Do I really need to explain what I'd get out of giving you a sponge bath?"

My shoulders dropped. Why was I constantly waiting for him to remember? I should've been happy *this* Drew decided to come around. *This* Drew was trying to make amends. *This* Drew wanted my forgiveness.

"Has your PT got you doing leg raises?" His voice snapped me out of my head.

"Yup."

"How about floor slides?"

I nodded.

"Good. When does she think you'll be full weight-bearing?"

I shrugged. "She said it's up to me."

"So tomorrow?"

I snorted. "I wish. But I'm driven. I'll do whatever it takes."

He nodded, his voice lowered. "I know."

My eyes focused out the passenger window at the passing buildings. I could do it. I could have a conversation with him like he was just an old friend. Not the person who took me off the track. Not the person I let in just to be let down by him in the end. "So what's next for you?" I looked back to him.

He shrugged. "I've still got to take my Boards, but I've been looking online for PT positions in the area."

Every muscle in my body tensed. "So that's why you came by today? Trying to get a job?"

He shook his head. "The only thing that brought me there was you." He looked me dead in the eyes. "*You.*"

There went the damn flutters.

His eyes jumped between the road and me. "I want to know you."

I huffed out my aggravation. Why was I angry at the thought of him using me for a job? Why was I pissed he wanted to know me better? Why was my body continually betraying my head? "What do you want to know?"

"Everything I don't already know."

I crossed my arms. "And what is it you think you already know?"

"Lots of things."

My cynical brow lifted. "Like what?"

"You love candy."

"Oh, big surprise there. Not only have you seen me eat it, but it's a known fact that every girl loves sweets, especially when PMSing."

His eyes continued jumping between the road and me. "You're loyal to a fault. Sticking by everyone else when they need you, but having very few people you can rely on."

A bout of déjà vu swept over me. "So, what are you saying? I need a shrink or Match.com?"

He shook his head. "I just gave you a compliment, which you're clearly pathetic at taking."

My eyes widened in mock outrage. "Am not."

He pulled to a stop and threw the truck into park, jumping out before I even realized we were in front of my building. He pulled open my door but blocked my exit. "You're beautiful."

My face fell into a grimace. "What?"

"You've got the most beautiful blue eyes. They twinkle like a kid's on Christmas morning when you like something. Usually food."

My eyes cast down. I knew what he was doing. And I'd accept his compliments if it was the last thing I did.

"And your lips." He grasped the top of the doorframe. "They're so damn kissable I think about doing it every day like some horny teenager."

A blush crept up my neck and into my cheeks. I could feel it all the way down to my toes.

"And your skin. It's so damn—"

"*Gah!*" My breath burst out of me. "Stop it. I get it. I can't take a compliment. Fine. Now back up."

He stepped back with a small grin and helped me onto the sidewalk and to the door. "Let me help you inside."

I shook my head, suddenly remembering we didn't have a comfortable relationship anymore. "I've got it."

"You're stubborn. You know that, right?"

I nodded, knowing it was both a strength and a curse. "Add it to the list. Thanks for the ride."

"I'll be here tomorrow at ten-thirty. Don't leave without me."

I stared into his sincere eyes for a long moment. It wasn't fair for me to lead him on. To give him false hope for a reconciliation. "I can't do this, Drew."

His brows inverted. "Do what? Let me take you to therapy?"

I shook my head. "You know what I mean."

He took a couple steps back from me. "No, I don't. I want you, Andi. I won't hide that. And I'll be damned if you don't let me fight for you. You might've given up on the possibility of us, but I haven't. I could see it in your eyes today. You want to forgive me. You want to let yourself be free of the anger and hate you feel toward me." He took one step closer, hesitant to get too close. "It's okay to forgive me. You don't have to forget. I'm not asking you to. I don't deserve that. But we *both* deserve to be happy. Why not do it together? This." He motioned his hand between us. "Us being at odds. It's not helping either of us. Try, Andi. Try to forgive me."

I stared across the space between us. He'd laid it all out there. I'd give him that. But there were still so many conflicted thoughts running through my head. So many feelings I didn't know what to do with.

So what did I do?

Nothing.

Nothing but maneuver myself inside my building and try to forget about the one guy who was making it impossible to forget about him.

CHAPTER NINETEEN

I'd spent the hours since Drew dropped me off staring at my blank television screen. Replaying his words over and over again in my head. Trying to convince myself to forgive him for hurting me. For keeping the truth from me. For turning my world upside down. But trying to convince myself to forgive him and actually forgiving him were two completely different things. Maybe with time I'd forget the pain he'd caused. But right now—

A knock on my door pulled me from my head.

I pushed myself up from the sofa nervous he'd shown up again. Nervous that if he confronted me again, he'd push me to make a decision. And if that were the case, he'd be unhappy with the decision.

I hobbled to the door and grasped the knob. "Who is it?"

There was a brief pause. "Brock."

WTF?

I pulled open the door to find my ex standing in the doorway holding a big bouquet of flowers in a glass vase. "Hey."

I winced at the sight of his shaggy blonde hair and too tanned skin. Our last interaction months before had left me with a broken heart and him with a black eye. "What are you doing here?"

His weight shifted from left to right, a habit that drove me nuts. "I just wanted to see you."

My nose scrunched in disgust. "Why?"

He held out the vase. "Here."

I took the heavy vase from him. "You do realize I couldn't even get you to buy me flowers on Valentine's Day when we were dating."

He shrugged. "Things change. Can I come in?"

"Why?"

He laughed. "I want to check in. See how you're doing." He stepped forward, giving me no other option than to step back so he could enter.

I closed the door and watched as he moved around my apartment. Though he'd been there a hundred times, it was odd having him back in my space. He didn't fit anymore. "You didn't have to come over. A text would've been fine."

"Why? We're friends."

I snorted as I carried the vase over to the island.

"Andi," he groaned.

I spun around to face him. "Look, no need to rehash the past. I'm over it. It's just hard seeing you here being sympathetic when you weren't when I was in one piece."

He leaned against the back of the sofa and crossed his arms. "People screw up. I screwed up. But I should still be allowed to visit you when you're hurt."

"And I should be allowed to give you shit for waiting almost two months to do it."

He huffed out a sigh. "Look, I knew Logan would be by your side."

I nodded. "She was."

"I'm sorry about the Olympics."

I averted my gaze as tears prickled the backs of my eyes. Brock knew how hard I trained to qualify. He knew running was my life.

"Hey," he said softly. "Look at me."

I closed my eyes and purged my tears before looking up at him.

"Life sucks."

I choked on a laugh as I dropped down onto one of the kitchen stools. "That's an understatement. And coming from you, quite comical."

"I deserve that."

A long pause passed between us.

"She made it."

Brock's brows furrowed. "Who?"

"Marley. She took my spot on the team."

He nodded. "I heard. If it's any consolation, she wasn't bragging all over campus about it."

"Well at least there's that."

"Yeah. Strange though, right?"

"Yeah. The girl's got the biggest mouth on campus."

He cocked his head. "It might be a tie with Logan."

I grinned. "That's true."

"She's been a good friend, though, hasn't she?"

"Yup. And you suck."

Given the flicker in his eyes, he completely agreed with me. "We both know you're better off without me. My head's all over the place."

I winced at the double meaning. "Yeah. That's the reason we broke up."

His eyes narrowed before he caught on and laughed to himself. "Half the time I don't know if I'm coming or going."

I winced again. "I find it hard to believe you don't know if you're coming. Guys are kind of all about that, aren't they?" I raised a brow.

He threw back his head and burst into laughter. "Some things will never change with you."

I smiled. And for the first time in a long time, I felt my hatred toward him dissipating. What good had it done me anyway? He'd moved on and so had I. It wasn't like I wanted him back. He'd forever just be some guy I dated, who broke my heart, and was never really right for me to begin with. We've all got one.

"Seriously, though," he continued. "I wasn't ready for anything serious when we were together."

"Yeah. I kind of figured that with the cheating thing."

He shrugged. "A guy just knows when he's ready to settle down. I wasn't."

I cocked my head to the side. "Ever think of letting me know?"

"I think my problem was I knew you were the right girl. You drink like a champ, can swear with the best of them, and are as sexy as hell. And in a few years when I'm ready to commit, I'll probably be kicking myself for letting you go." He shrugged. "You just came around at the wrong time."

As screwed up as his rationale sounded, in a messed up sort of way it made sense. Don't get me wrong. It wouldn't have sat well with me right after we broke up. When the hurt was so deep. So raw. Nothing would have. But now, when I didn't feel the same hatred toward him, it did.

And, as shocking as it was to admit, Brock was right about one thing. Timing *was* everything in life. I was someone who knew that all too well.

"Sure, some guys may never be ready to settle down," he added. "But others will do it when they find the one they're willing to fight to hold onto. The one they'd die before giving up on."

I nodded, wondering when the hell my asshole ex-boyfriend had become so wise.

* * *

"I'm so happy you called," Logan yelled over the loud music. "I miss girls' night out." She threw back her tequila shot and slammed it back down on our high top table like a rock star.

"I know." I threw back my own shot. It was funny how pain disappeared after a shitload of beer and too many shots.

"Woo-hoo!" Logan shouted, drawing attention from half the men in the bar, most of whom already noticed her too short skirt and too tight top.

I didn't have to worry about getting attention. Forget my days in hooker heels. Anyone who noticed my black plunging neckline or short skirt, instantly noticed the boot accessorizing my foot and wrote me off as a capable dance partner or hook-up.

"So Brock?" Logan lifted a brow. "I can't believe he had the balls to show up at your place."

I laughed. "No kidding."

"And why the hell did he wait so long?"

I nodded toward her. "Probably scared you'd kick his ass."

"Damn straight I would," she laughed. "He was always such a prick."

I nodded. "Why do we always fall for the pricks?"

Logan's eyes cast down. "Not always."

I could sense her need to talk. Her need to disclose what had been bothering her. I'd been so consumed with everything going on with me, so wrapped up in my misery, I hadn't been the friend she needed me to be. *That stopped now.* "Are you ever gonna tell me what happened with Luke—I mean Avery?"

She shrugged. "Things didn't work out."

"Oh?"

She picked up her beer and took a long swig. "He said he couldn't stand competing for my attention with all my fans. *Fans?* Can you even believe he said that?"

I stared across the table at my beautiful friend. "Logan, I know you're not blind. Look around. Half the guys in this place are waiting for you to drop something so they have a reason to come over here."

"More like get a good look at my vagina."

"Well, that, too."

Her blonde curls whipped around. You name it. Biker. Frat guy. Businessman. Their eyes were glued to her. Ogling her. Willing her toward them.

"You have your pick."

"I know that," she snapped.

I couldn't really fault her for her self-confidence. After years of garnering excessive male attention, she wasn't blind or stupid. She knew they were looking. And she knew exactly what they wanted. It was probably the reason she never committed.

"It's just…this time, I only wanted him. It wasn't about the chase anymore. I didn't care what else was out there. I just liked being with him."

"Have you told him?"

She raised a brow. I hated that brow. "Have you told Drew?"

Ignoring her question, I chugged down my beer, welcoming the cool liquid and its anticipated mind-numbing effects.

Logan leaned back in her stool and crossed her arms, waiting me out.

Dammit.

When I lowered the bottle, my eyes scanned the testosterone-filled room. Why couldn't I meet a guy here? One who had no baggage? One who wouldn't hurt me? One who *hadn't* hurt me?

"So?" she pressed.

I took a swig of beer and forced my eyes back to hers. "What do you want to hear?"

"For starters, that you want to have his football-playing babies."

I choked on my drink.

"Because if you don't, if you really want nothing to do with him, you need to tell him. He won't chase you if he thinks there's no hope. The guy's got more pride than that."

"Maybe he'd stop chasing me if you stopped telling him where I am." I couldn't disguise the exasperation in my voice. "I'm surprised he hasn't shown up here."

She picked up her phone and held it out to me. "Call him. Tell him to leave you alone."

I stared down at her phone, wondering if I possessed the nerve to do it. To actually send him away. To guarantee we never saw each other again. Would I be okay with that? Would it hurt to lose him for a second—no third time? Was there anything even worth salvaging?

I shook my head, which only garnered one of Logan's mega-watt, told-you-so smiles. But that disappeared the moment I pulled my own phone from my handbag. "His number's in my contacts."

Her eyes widened. She didn't think I'd do it. But there I sat, scrolling through names until I found his. I lifted the phone to my ear.

"Hi." Drew answered, seemingly excited by my call.

"Hey," my voice slurred. *This had bad written all over it.*

"It's pretty late. Is everything okay?"

What was I doing? I met Logan's eyes. They were locked on mine. "Yeah. Everything's fine. I'm just out with Logan."

"Are you drinking?" Drew asked, his voice filled with amusement.

"A little."

"Uh huh. Do you want me to come by?"

My eyes shot wide. I held down the phone and covered it with my hand. "He wants to know if he should come by."

She lifted her chin toward my phone. "You do know you're covering the wrong end, right?"

I grimaced, lifting the phone back to my ear. "Drew?"

"I'm here, Andi." Why did it sound like he was laughing?

"I just wanted to tell you—ask you—if you…well if you were still picking me up in the morning?"

"I said I would."

"Okay."

"But Andi…" His voice practically purred. "You could save me a trip and have me over now. That way I'd already be there in the morning."

I swallowed down a grapefruit-sized knot. "Um, no. Tomorrow's fine."

"You don't sound so sure."

"I'm sure," I said way too quickly.

"If you say so."

"Drew?"

"Yes, Andi?"

I paused for a long time. Most people would have hung up after the prolonged dead air, but not Drew. He'd wait for me to end the call. Everything that happened between us was now in my court. Every decision. Every interaction. If he truly meant what he told me, he wouldn't risk screwing it up. "Goodnight."

I could hear the smile in his voice. "Goodnight."

I tapped off my phone and slid it across the table like it was about to detonate. "Fuck."

Logan burst out laughing.

"What did I just do?"

"I believe you did *not* send him packing. If anything, you just gave him a reason to stay."

I dropped my face into my hands. "Am I nuts?"

"No, you're human. And he's hot."

I spread my fingers so I could see through them. "I think a small part of me—a very small part—might want to have his football-playing babies."

"I knew it!" Logan jumped to her feet. "Another round of shots over here, bartender!"

* * *

The taxi dropped me off in front of my condo sometime after one in the morning. Forget the boot on my foot. With the amount of liquor I'd consumed, I was amazed I could even put one foot in front of the other. Had Logan not been nearly passed out in the backseat, she would've helped me to the door. Then again, I probably would've refused her help. I don't know why I found it so difficult to let others help me.

I handed the female driver enough cash to cover both Logan and me, then hobbled to the entrance. I slid my key card through the slot and stepped inside the building.

"Hey," a deep voice startled the hell out of me.

I spun faster than I thought possible with my boot on. Drew stood against the inside wall with his arms crossed. "What are you doing here?" I slurred.

Fan-freaking-tastic.

"Well," he pushed off the wall and stalked closer.

Why was I enjoying the fact that he stalked me like prey?

Stupid alcohol.

"I wanted to make sure you got home safely. By the sound of it, you had a lot to drink."

"Did not."

A crooked smile tipped his lips. "Okay."

I moved to step around him but my boot caught on the carpet. If not for Drew's quick reflexes and strong grasp on my arm, I would've face-planted.

He didn't release my arm. If anything, his grip tightened. "Let me help you upstairs."

I pulled my arm free. "I'm fine." I hated myself for being so pissy.

"I know you're fine," he explained. "But I want to help you upstairs."

I stared into his eyes, looking for a hidden agenda. Looking for a sign that I should turn and run far away from him—figuratively speaking of course. But all I saw were pretty emerald flecks. Lots of them.

Gahhhh.

"Okay."

A slow, heart-stopping smile slid across his lips.

Once I'd unlocked my door and stepped inside my condo, I spun to stop him from entering. As much as I liked that he'd shown up, I couldn't be trusted alone with him with so much alcohol running through my veins and tainting my judgment. "Well, goodnight. Again."

He stared across the small distance between us with his smile set firmly in place. "Goodnight. Again."

I gripped the door and began to close it. I would have succeeded had the toe of his shoe not stopped it. My eyes shot up.

He stepped closer. His big hands grasped my cheeks. Before I could stop him, his lips sealed over mine. I tried to resist. I really did. But the second his tongue ran across the seam of my lips, I was a drunken goner, parting my lips and giving myself over to raw desire. His eager tongue dove inside. I arched into him, wrapping my arms around his neck and walking him into my living room.

His hands dropped from my cheeks to my hips, his fingertips digging possessively into the flesh beneath my skirt. The door slammed with the pressure of his shoe, and within seconds, my back landed on the sofa. Drew followed me down, settling carefully between my legs while continuing his attack on my lips. A delicious shiver rocked through me as his lips shifted, trailing slow sensual kisses down my neck.

My head tipped back on a moan, the kiss shooting straight to the ball of nerves between my thighs.

He pulled back, his breathing ragged and his chest heaving as fiercely as my own. "Tell me you want me."

I stared up into his earnest eyes. Was that how I felt? Did I want him, with all his flaws and shortcomings? Could I be with him knowing the circumstances that brought us together? My drunken mind said, "Hell yeah." But was it the truth? Was it what I really wanted in the light of day with a clear mind?

I gazed up at the worry lines pinching his brows. Not forgiving him was hurting me and completely tearing him apart.

He closed his eyes and dropped his forehead to mine. "Tell me how to do this, Andi. Tell me how to make this better. Tell me what I need to do to be with you."

The pain in his voice destroyed every last bit of reserve inside of me. He'd bared his soul to me. He'd promised to fight for me, and there he was doing just that. I needed to either accept him as he was—after what he'd done—or send him packing. This indecision was torture. For both of us.

Ah, hell.

I grasped his cheeks, forcing him to look at me. I had no clue what to say. What to do. I just knew I didn't want him hurting anymore. Hurting sucked. And we'd both done too much of it.

"Tell me this isn't all one-sided," he whispered.

Staring into his sad eyes, my head somehow meshed with my heart, at least for the time being. I shook my head. "It isn't."

He exhaled a giant breath. "I'm so damn sorry." He captured my lips. I could feel his relief, his happiness, his need for me as his tongue caressed deep inside my mouth. Sweeping. Owning. Empowering. If only I could hold on to the moment. If only I could shove down the blame long enough to let him in. If only I could forgive him whole-heartedly and mean it.

When he finally pulled back, his pupils were dilated. "I want you so much right now."

"I want you, too." Stupid, *stupid* alcohol.

He lifted himself off of me and stood. I looked up at him towering over me with his hand extended. "Show me your room."

I grabbed hold of his hand. He pulled me up, cautious of my leg. I didn't let up my hold, just led him down the short hallway to my bedroom. Once inside I turned to him. His eyes smoldered. Smoldered in a way I'd only ever dreamed a guy would look at me. With want. With need. With desire for me and only me.

I dropped my hands to the hem of my top and lifted. He stopped me at my bra and tugged my shirt back down.

"Not tonight. Not like this."

My shoulders dropped on a childish huff. "You do realize this is the second time you're turning me down."

With the gentle touch of his finger, he lifted my chin. "It is taking *all* the willpower I have right now not to attack you. So please stop acting like I just killed your cat."

"I hate cats."

His lips spread into a grin. "You know what I mean."

The chances of me even remembering what was happening were slim at best. If he really wanted this, he should've taken advantage of my drunkenness. The morning might've been a completely different story.

He linked his fingers with mine and moved me to the bed, urging me to sit. He knelt on the floor in front of me and unhitched the straps on my boot, gently slipping my foot out of it. When he stood back up, he reached over his shoulder and tugged his shirt over his head.

Sweet Jesus.

Him standing there in my bedroom, in all his bare-chested glory, was a fantasy brought to life. Not to mention, making abstaining painfully difficult. I closed my eyes, willing myself to relax. To slow down my jittery mind. My pounding heart.

That's when a powerful gust of déjà vu swept over me.

The beach-themed bedroom. Drew at the foot of the bed. *This* Drew. His eyes raking over me after carrying me inside from the rain and ocean. After telling me he wanted moments like this with me. Those memories were ones he and I shared. Not memories of a Drew who never existed.

I shook off the recollection, bringing me back to the here and now. And right here, right now, Drew stripped down to his boxers and moved forward, causing me to lie back on my bed. He scooted down beside me and moved me so my head rested on my pillow and my legs extended down the length of the bed. Rolling me gently away from him onto my side, he snuggled up behind me, his hard chest pressing into my back. He wrapped his arms around my waist and pulled me closer into him. "Tonight, we sleep. In the morning—"

"We go at it like rabbits?"

He buried his nose in my hair and laughed. "Fuck, yeah."

CHAPTER TWENTY

I woke to strong arms holding my back to what felt like a brick wall. Gentle kisses trailed down the back of my neck and over my shoulder.

My eyes snapped open. The sun's early morning rays glowed behind my closed window blinds. Faint recollections of the previous night swirled in my head, none actually slowing down enough to become full visions.

Who was in my bed?

Why was he kissing me?

His arms loosened and his hands slipped to my sides, moving up and down the fabric covering my hips. Why was I still in my skirt? "Morning," Drew purred.

Memories bombarded me all at once. Me calling him. Him coming by. Me trying to get naked. Him stopping me.

Oh, God.

"What's going through that head of yours?" he asked with laughter in his raspy morning voice. "I can practically hear the gears grinding."

"Ummm."

His breath hitched. His hands on my hips stopped moving. "You don't remember last night." It wasn't a question. It was the stark reality of the situation.

"Kind of?"

His entire body jerked back so we were no longer touching. "Fuck."

"We definitely didn't do that." I flipped over, momentarily floored by how gorgeous he looked shirtless and ruffled in my bed. "Why?"

He raked his fingers through his hair, his eyes burning into mine. "I wouldn't take advantage of you like that." His voice dripped with disgust at the thought of it. "If it happens, you need to be one hundred percent alert and on board."

I nodded, my mind searching for something to say. Anything to stop the awkwardness surrounding us.

"Tell me what you're thinking." Drew's words were serious, nervous even.

I wanted to be honest, but having him so close made honesty so much more difficult. I averted my gaze. "I don't know how I'm supposed to forget. I want to. I really do. But for so long my Olympic dream was my only dream." My eyes slid back to his. "So the fact that it's gone, and you're the one who took it away...the two thoughts are constantly jockeying for space in my brain. When I try to push them away, I'm left with emptiness. And *nothing* is making me happy."

He nodded. I knew it was tough for him to hear, but he needed to know how confusing it was to be me.

"I appreciate what you've been trying to do. And I'd like to believe you're doing it for me and not to ease your own guilty conscious." Tears prickled the backs of my eyes. "But I just...I just don't know."

I expected him to move away, grab his clothes, and leave. But he didn't. Instead, he slowly moved closer, wrapping his arms around me and urging me against his chest. I rested my cheek against his warm skin and listened to his heart's rhythmic beat. I wondered if it always raced that quickly or if my words had affected him.

We didn't speak. We just lay there in our own heads, yet again.

What I couldn't grasp, was how the one person who brought me the most pain in my life, was the only person who seemed to soothe it.

"I wish I wasn't your biggest mistake," he said.

His comment blew all my thoughts out of my head. "You're not."

He scoffed.

"I just wish you could've gotten out of the draft some other way." No matter how hard I tried to reel them back, tears escaped my eyes, slipping down my cheeks and onto his bare chest. It's what I'd been holding back saying. What I'd been holding off admitting. Because while he destroyed my dreams in that one selfish moment, he almost lost his own life.

His *life*.

It wasn't just about me and what I lost. It was about his need to hurt himself. His desperation. His loneliness.

"I was weak." His voice cracked with emotion. "I *am* weak."

"You were scared and alone. You had no one to help you."

"I wish I had you."

I expelled a long breath. "Me, too."

I could feel his body shift and him look down at me. "Andi?"

I lifted my head, resting my chin on his chest. I must've been a horrid sight with tears and mascara trailing down my cheeks as I stared up at him.

"I want to deserve you." He brushed his thumb across my cheek, sweeping away the tears. "I want to be everything you need and everything you don't have. I want to be someone you never have to question. Someone you trust. Someone you could love for the rest of your life."

I closed my eyes, his words stinging and elating at the same time. How could both emotions be so strong? How could I be so conflicted? The sincerity in his eyes and his words were enough to send me over the edge. But I'd already been there.

I opened my eyes and rolled off his chest, needing some distance. Needing it to all make sense. His words. His feelings. His actions. I propped myself up on my elbow. Now we were at eye-level, and I could gauge his response. His honesty. "Why me?"

His eyes narrowed. "Why not you?"

"Come on, Drew. I've heard the stories from Avery. I've made you work. You have girls who don't. What is it about me?"

I didn't think it was possible, but his eyes narrowed even more. "Do you not get how amazing you are?"

I tilted my head. "Bullshit."

His head shot back. "I'm serious."

I eyed him unconvinced. "I've got nowhere to be." I wasn't fishing for compliments. If he was so convinced he needed me, that I was the one, I needed to understand where it stemmed from.

"I told you at the beach house. You're persistent. I like that you won't give up on me—and before you say it, you may like to think you have, but I know deep down you haven't."

"The nurses and doctors never gave up on you. Why me, Drew?"

He pulled in a frustrated breath. "I like that you don't put up with my shit. That you don't let me get away with anything. You call me on it."

"So does Avery. Why do you want *me*?"

He closed his eyes. Was he pondering the question or coming up with a winning response? "You cared about me when no one else did." When his eyes opened, sincerity not dishonesty shaded them. "You didn't have to. You weren't getting anything out of it. You just did. And as much as you probably want to deny that, too, you did care, Andi. I could hear it in your voice. See it in your frustration with me. Feel it in your hesitance to keep coming back."

"Betty showed up," I reminded him, the recollection still twisting my insides. "She seemed to care."

"You're right. She *seemed* to care. They all seem to care. But none of them do. None of them will be around now that I'm not going pro. None of them are you."

I shook my head. There had to be more to it. More to his unwavering certainty. "I'm not convinced."

"God dammit, woman," he growled in exasperation. "You not being in my life isn't an option." He looked me dead in the eyes to be sure I was paying attention. I *was* paying attention, hanging on every word. "It's always been you. Since I woke up and saw you sitting there holding my hand, I knew it was you."

"But can't you see how that doesn't make sense to me? We're practically strangers."

He scoffed. "I guess it wouldn't make sense. I'm the one who had the dreams."

My entire face scrunched in confusion. "What dreams?"

"When I was unconscious, I had these dreams. They didn't feel like dreams. More like memories."

My skin tightened as my heartbeat sped up. "What kind of memories?"

"Us...on a rooftop..." His squinting eyes and hesitation showed someone searching their subconscious for details that had become hazy. "Eating pizza..." His eyes drifted to the ceiling like he knew none of it made any sense. "Doing shots."

I could hardly breathe for fear of stopping what was happening.

"You told me you hated me, but I knew you didn't mean it. Then I was giving you..."

"Giving me what?" I whispered.

I noticed an emotion I rarely saw in his eyes. Embarrassment. "A sponge bath."

My breath rushed out of me like a gust of wind. "Oh my God."

I wasn't crazy.

I *knew* I wasn't crazy.

Misinterpreting my response, Drew gazed sadly back at me. "I know it doesn't make any sense."

A cross between a laugh and a sob escaped me. "It does." I reached over and cupped his cheeks between my shaking hands. "As crazy as it sounds, it does."

"How can you even say that?"

I took a deep breath, filling my lungs to capacity while working up the nerve to tell him the truth. I released my breath slowly. "I had dreams, too."

His brows dipped. "What?"

I shrugged. "I knew things I couldn't possibly know. About you. About us. Before we ever even met."

His mouth opened. Then closed. Then opened again. "You're serious?"

I nodded. "My doctor assured me they were hallucinations caused by the edema. But then your nurse told me...well...she had other theories. Strange theories I never seriously considered. But now that you're telling me you had them, too..." I shook my head. "I have no idea what to believe anymore."

"Why didn't you tell me?" he asked.

"Why didn't you tell *me*?"

"I thought I was crazy. I didn't want to end up in a padded room. I was taking it to the grave."

I dropped my forehead to his and closed my eyes. "I wish you'd told me."

"It was just so fucked up. And add to it the fact that you wanted nothing to do with me. I *made* you want nothing to do with me. Everything was a mess."

I still couldn't believe it. Margie's words swirled around my head. Could I really allow myself to believe there was something else at play? Something bigger than the both of us that brought us together in the first place? "This is so nuts." I pulled back so I could see him. "But at least now we don't have to be crazy alone."

He blinked hard. "We don't?"

The hopeful look in his eyes sent a burst of realization washing over me. "That's how you knew. That's why you've been so sure about us."

His lips pulled to the side as he nodded. "But I need you to know, those dreams might've been what initially made me feel close to you. But it was your stubbornness and determination to break through my walls that made me know you were the one person who would stick around *for* me. Not because you expected something *from* me. It's what made me know you were special. You *are* special, Andi. That's how I knew giving up on us was never an option."

My heart flipped over in my chest.

"And when I tried to push you away, it was because I was angry. Angry I was the one who hurt you. Angry you were the one who got caught in the middle of my mess. Angry I'd fallen for the one girl I'd never be able to have."

I slipped my hands to the sides of his head, tunneling my fingers into the hair there. I tilted my head, noticing his boyish features for the first time. The features of a son who hadn't been loved the way a son should've been loved. The features of an athlete who had too much pressure placed on him when it was the last thing he wanted. The features of a guy who couldn't be sure who to trust since everyone in his life wanted something from him. "You do have me, Drew. I'm right here."

His brows pulled together, his vulnerability almost too much to take. "But I want you for longer than just right now."

I nodded. "I know."

He stared at me like I'd lost my flipping mind. "I think you might still be drunk."

I shook my head. "For the first time in a long time, I think my head's a little less foggy. And I'm starting to feel more than just pain."

"You can't be sure."

Was he really trying to dissuade me? After everything he'd said to convince me? After telling me about his dreams? I nodded. "I am."

"This won't be easy. I can be a real asshole."

"No kidding," I laughed.

He leveled me with those gorgeous green eyes. "But I want this. And I'm willing to work like hell for it."

I dragged my teeth over my bottom lip and nodded. "Me, too."

His smile spread wide as he moved in slowly—so slowly I thought he'd never make it to me. "And I want *you*," he assured me, before finally pressing his lips to mine, slow yet forceful. This kiss carried relief. Resolution. The possibility of a future together.

He pulled back, nuzzling his nose against mine. His fingertips coasted over my healed cheek. His eyes zoned in on the spot, undoubtedly remembering where my scratch sat and how it got there.

"Hey." My fingers tunneled through the hair at his nape. "I'm okay. I'm good. We're good."

His eyes moved from my cheek to my eyes, instantly softening. "We are good. And we're going to be so good together."

"You think?"

"I *know*." The deep rasp in his voice gave me an immediate burst of courage, completely turning me on.

"I really liked the Drew in my dreams."

His lips kicked up in the corner. "He's still around."

"How about the one from the beach house?"

He nodded. "He's around, too."

I smirked. "The one who brought me gummy worms and took me to the track?"

He snickered. "Here."

I sat up. Drew eyed me curiously. "So, if they're all present and accounted for…" I tugged my shirt over my head. "Does that mean someone will have the nerve to get past first base?" I tossed it to the floor.

His tongue shot out, gliding over his bottom lip as his hungry eyes dropped to my lacy black bra. "Oh, I'd say at least second."

I reached down and pushed my skirt down my legs, tossing it to the floor. "How about if I'm aiming for third?"

"At this rate, sweetheart, you can have whatever the fuck you want." Drew shoved down his boxers with a grin.

"So a homerun's in the cards?" I laughed.

"I think you're forgetting. I'm a football guy. We speak in terms of tackle." He lunged playfully forward, forcing me onto my back and following me down. "Offsides." His big strong hands gripped my sides, his fingers digging in as they slid from my bra all the way down to my hips. "First and ten." His fingers moved to the elastic on each leg of my underwear, tracing them down slowly, the light touch of his fingers leaving a glorious path of numbness in their wake. "Maybe a quarterback sneak." His middle finger slipped underneath my underwear and inside the wet folds he'd created. "Or a safety." My head pushed back into the pillow as his finger glided slowly back and forth.

The anticipation of what he'd do next added to the hum taking over my body. It took every bit of effort not to groan as his finger slipped back and forth. Without warning he added another finger, creating the same glorious sensations before pushing them inside. As his fingers thrust in and out of me, he used his thumb to circle my throbbing nub.

Good, God.

I lifted my hips, bucking him slightly—unsure if I was trying to ride his hand or get him inside me faster. "I believe they call this an interception," I said breathless.

His lips turned up, keen to my needs. "Actually, it's called rushing the passer."

I laughed. "Well, any chance we'll be moving toward a touchdown?"

"This isn't a race."

"Or a game of football, but I've still been playing nice."

With a smile, his fingers slipped out of me.

Ugh. Maybe I shouldn't have rushed the passer.

His knee carefully spread my legs further apart. "We've got all the time in the world," he promised, pressing his hard length into my center.

"Oh, you think so, huh?" I grasped his cheeks between my hands and pulled his mouth down to mine, moving my lips urgently as his hips lazily pushed against me. A shiver rolled through me as my hands slipped to the back of his head and tightened in his hair. I urged him closer—deeper, licking away at his mouth like I planned to devour him whole. "Pull them down," I said against his lips.

I let my hands fall away as he sat back on his knees, tugging my panties down and tossing them on the floor. He leaned off the bed and grabbed his jeans from the same spot and dug into the pocket. Finding what he needed, he ripped the small packet open with his teeth.

I watched as he rolled on the condom, enjoying the show more than I ever had before. But with Drew's amazing body, and the way every muscle swelled when he moved, how could I not be enthralled—and horny as hell?

I beckoned him back with my index finger, trying my best to be the seductress I wasn't even remotely close to being. A devilish glint flashed in his eyes as he crawled back over me, his body covering mine. This time I felt his entire body from head to toe as he buried his face in my neck, pressing open-mouthed kisses along my skin. I felt his hardened length slip between my legs, coasting over the wetness there.

My head fell back on a gasp and my body buzzed with pleasure. I could tell he wanted to prolong it. Wanted to take his time. Wanted me to enjoy the sensation every time he slipped over me without entering. Every time he purposely hit the ball of nerves at the apex of my thighs and my body trembled. Again. And again.

My fingertips dug into the smooth skin on his sides, moving to his hips, trying to hang on and enjoy the pleasure he brought to every part of my body. But soon, his quest to bring me pleasure turned to torture. And every slip, every kiss, every touch of his hands on my skin became too intense. Too mind-numbing. Too much.

I thrust my hips up. "*Drewww.* I can't take anymore."

He pulled back and looked into my eyes. "See, that's where I think you're wrong." He purposely dipped inside my warmth and coasted along, teasing me with the feeling of things to come. "I think you can take a lot more."

I closed my eyes and inhaled a deep breath, trying to enjoy his playfulness and every magnificent pass of his erection.

"See," he said all raspy and sexy. "I knew you could do it."

"I hate you," I lied, as my body threatened to self-combust.

"I don't believe you," he murmured, his hips continuing their glorious movements.

My eyes popped opened. "Please, Drew." *Yup. That was a whine.* "Stop."

"Stop?" Every part of his body stopped moving. "Is that what you really want?" He rolled off, lying beside me with his head in his palm and his massive bicep flexed and bulging in my face.

Was it weird I wanted to lick it? "I meant stop torturing me," I panted.

"I didn't realize I was torturing you." He said it all innocently, but seriously? After what he'd just been doing, he was anything but innocent.

Bastard.

I rolled to my side and reached around my back, unsnapping the clasp on my bra. *Two can play that game.* I reached back around and pulled the bra off, tossing it on the floor. I rested my head in my palm and waited him out.

His eyes dropped to my chest. *No big surprise there.* Then they lifted almost immediately to my eyes. That's when I saw it. His fierce desire. His want. His need. His realization that I was his for the taking. That's all it took. He tackled me onto my back, caging me in with his forearms beside my head. "Woman, you're gonna be the death of me." His hips pushed once, giving me the much need tremor I yearned for. Then, without any more teasing, he thrust inside, sheathing himself deep to my core.

Groaning, I arched into him, my breasts rubbing against his hard chest. My fingers slid down his back, over his taut muscles, trailing down to the deep curve at the base of his spine that led to his perfect ass. My nails dug into his smooth skin, pulling him closer into me, loving the feel of him pounding away at me. Time after time.

"God," he rasped into my neck. "What are you doing to me?"

"Letting you slide into home," I panted.

"You're forgetting. Quarterbacks score touchdowns." The growl in his voice and the feel of his body stretching mine wide sent me climbing to the peak. "Fuck the extra point. This right here, this is what we call a two point conversion." He reached down and flicked his thumb where I ached for it most.

Once. Twice. Three times. And I was careening over the crest. A tremor tore through my body, stealing my breath. Aftershocks zapped at every nerve ending, tingling to the tips of my fingertips and toes. My head fell back as I gasped for air.

Drew continued thrusting until his body stilled and tremors rocked through him. His weight lowered onto me. *All* his weight. And I loved the feel of every rock hard inch of him as our chests heaved. Our breaths huffed. Our hearts raced. We were one. And for the first time in a long freaking time, I had hope. Hope that I'd found someone who'd deliver on his promises. Hope that I was enough to make him stick around. Hope that this was the last Drew—the only Drew—I'd have to contend with in this lifetime.

CHAPTER TWENTY-ONE

I gazed out the passenger window of Drew's truck feeling completely at ease. More than I'd been in a very long time. After picking me up from physical therapy, I assumed he planned to take me home. But the roads he took brought us closer and closer to the coast.

My head whipped toward him. "Where are we going?"

His eyes jumped from the road to me. He looked nervous. Hesitant. "I've got something to show you."

I twisted my ponytail around my finger. "After last night, I'm pretty sure I've seen it all."

He chuckled, but it held nervousness. Trepidation even. He pulled to a stop outside an abandoned storefront on one of the busier beach roads. The windows were blotted with white paint. No sign hung over the glass door, but a *For Lease* sign hung in its window.

Drew hopped out of his truck and hurried around to open my door. "Now I need you to have an open mind."

I nodded as he laced his fingers with mine and tugged me toward the door.

His free hand pulled a key from his pocket and jammed it into the lock.

"Why do you have a key?"

He unlocked the door and pushed it open, moving to the side to let me enter first.

I stepped into the center of a large empty room and spun around.

Drew followed me inside, closing the door behind him. "What do you think?"

"Of an empty room?" My voice echoed off the bare concrete walls.

"Of my rehab clinic?"

I stared across the room at him, the idea not processing completely.

"I want you to be my first patient."

My forehead creased. "You're opening a business?"

He nodded slowly, closely watching my reaction. "Once I pass my Boards, it's all mine."

I glanced around the vacant space. "You're opening your own business *here*?"

He nodded, his eyes boring into mine as if trying to read my thoughts.

I swallowed. Hard. "You really weren't going to leave?"

He shook his head. "When I want something, I'm willing to do whatever it takes to get it."

I crossed my arms and tilted my hips. "So you wanted to open your own business?"

"Yes." His lips quirked up in the corners as he walked toward me, his shoulders back and his arms swinging with purpose. "But I wanted you a hell of a lot more."

I fought back a smile. "I hate you."

He backed me into the concrete wall, caging me in with his hands beside my head. "You hate that you like me." As soon as the words left his lips, his head jolted back.

My eyes narrowed. "What's wrong?"

"I just had déjà vu."

I smiled. "I know the feeling."

"Oh, yeah?" His voice took on a suggestive tone.

I nodded, my eyes locked on his.

"Then do you already know what it's going to feel like when I make you very, very happy?" His face inched closer, prepared to make good on those words.

"Is this while you're rehabbing me or in bed?"

He cocked his head as his eyes dragged slowly down my body. "Both."

I laughed as he leaned toward my ear and dragged his teeth along my lobe, nibbling all the way around it. I tilted my head, giving him better access while I stared out at the empty space behind him. I envisioned the possibilities. Machines on the far side. A mirror along the opposite wall. Treadmills and bikes in the corner. Me on the weight bench with him on top of me. "So where do we start?"

"We?" he hummed against my ear.

"You don't think I'm gonna let you do this alone, do you?"

He pulled back and gazed down at me in what could only be described as admiration.

"I know," I said with a facetious smirk. "I'm a total keeper."

He moved in and kissed the smirk right off my lips. "Why do you think I've been trying to hang on to you?"

My eyes flashed away, unsure if I'd ever get used to his sincerity. "Think of all the clients you're gonna bring in because of your name."

"And my body."

I stifled a grin as I looked back at him. "Of course, there's always that."

He snickered. "No seriously. I'm banking on you."

"Me?"

"Yeah. Think of all the clients I'll bring in after getting *you* back on the track. And getting you a medal."

I slipped my arms around his waist and looked up into his eyes. "You really think I can do it?"

"You made me fall in love with you. So I'd say you're capable of anything."

My stomach became a fluttery mess. "So you love me?"

"Sweetheart, I fucking love everything about you, including this sarcastic mouth." He leaned in and kissed my lips, gently coaxing them apart with the swipe of his tongue, diving in and taking all of me. And of course I let him. Because for the first time, I trusted him. Whole-heartedly. He pulled back and shifted toward my neck, dragging his tongue all the way up to my ear. "And this tasty neck," he purred into my skin as his hands slipped around and squeezed my rear end. "And this ass," he growled. "God, I can't get enough of it."

"Nice to see someone's got their shit together," a deep voice interrupted, alerting us we weren't alone.

Drew and I froze, though our heads whipped toward the doorway. Avery turned on his heels and headed back outside. I buried my face in Drew's chest, laughing at what Avery overheard.

Drew lowered his lips to my ear. "He wanted us together almost as much as I did."

"Smart guy."

"Don't let him fool you. He definitely likes you. But with Avery, there's always an ulterior motive."

I pulled back, gazing up into the eyes of the guy who came along when I least expected him and turned my world upside down. I deserved to be happy. So did he. So did Avery. So did—

I glanced to the door with a slow-spreading grin. "Logan."

If Drew and I could get it together, there was no doubt in my mind that Avery and Logan could, too.

I looked back to Drew. "Oh, yeah. They're totally going to happen."

"Well, can they happen later? Because I've got plans for you and me and this big empty room."

"Oh, yeah?"

He lifted me up so I had no other option but to straddle his waist and lock my arms around his neck. "Oh, hell yeah."

EPILOGUE
Four Years Later
Italy

The shotgun fired, echoing throughout the packed stadium. My back foot pushed off the starting block. Every part of me focused on the finish line two laps away. Not my uncontrollable nerves. Not my over the top excitement. Not the other seven women vying for one of *my* medals. Yes, *my*. I wouldn't allow myself to believe otherwise.

I just needed to get to the end. And if my latest finish was any indication, I was in good position to place.

My feet slapped off the track as the momentum of my arms propelled me forward. As soon as I could get out of lane four, I wanted that front spot in lane one. I deserved that spot. It had been four long years in the making. And I'd be damned if anything else got in my way of achieving it. I'd come too far.

I rounded the first curve. My breathing was even. My adrenaline peaked. My heart crashing around inside my chest like a pinball. But none of it mattered. In less than two minutes, I'd know my fate.

Sure, it had been a long road. But I'd made it. And I didn't need to question how I'd gotten there. How I'd gotten back on my feet four years ago. How I'd pushed myself to train day after day.

The answer was easy. Drew.

He'd been my savior. He'd been my strength when I didn't have any. He'd been my confidence when I considered giving up. He'd been my motivator when I swore I'd never make it back.

Don't get me wrong. At times, he could still be a total asshole. But I knew how to handle that side of him. And when that ego of his got a little too big, I was right there to knock him down a peg or two. Because I loved him. I mean, he hadn't really given me any other choice.

Somewhere up in the massive crowd, probably somewhere he could see the entire track, Drew sat cheering with my parents and Logan. I could feel him down on the track. I could hear his words of encouragement. I could recite his constant praise as I trained my ass off to get back. And I could sense every bit of his unconditional love for me.

I hit the back straightaway and the break line, crossing over into the inside lane and into the middle of the pack. I trailed slightly behind three other runners. But that was fine. I'd planned for a slower first lap, saving all my energy for the second when I'd make my move.

I rounded the next curve, passing one of the runners. It felt good. I felt good. My knee and leg had fully recovered and were like brand new.

With every stride, I gained on the leaders. But my small victory was short-lived. Two other runners gained on me, passing me on my right.

Come on, Andi. You got this. You didn't come this far to finish in fifth place.

My body knew what it needed to do.

I entered the second lap, pushing myself into high gear.

This was the freaking Olympics. This was my dream.

My knees lifted higher. My arms pulled back further. My chest pressed out in an effort to lengthen my stride. My speed increased.

The breeze created by our motion blew against my sweaty face as I passed one runner. Then another.

You got this.

I tried to stay out of my head. I really did. But the two girls ahead of me weren't inches ahead; they were a couple strides ahead. I wouldn't be able to catch them. I knew that now.

But I didn't need the gold. My goal had always been a medal. And if I just kept up my pace and didn't let anyone else pass me, I would be a world champion.

I focused.

Focused on my form. Focused on the sounds of our feet clapping off the track. Focused on not getting tripped up in any of the other runners' feet.

As we rounded the final curve, the sounds of the crowd finally resonated. I'd been so focused on me and my journey, I hadn't thought of all the fans. All there to support their country. All there to cheer on their favorite athlete and see them bring home the medal.

But that's not why my parents, Logan, and Drew sat in that crowd. It's not why they flew thousands of miles. They sat there for *me*. They sat there to be *my* support system. They sat there to see *my* dream come to fruition.

And I couldn't let them down.

I *wouldn't* let them down.

I wouldn't let myself down.

I could see the finish line just meters away.

A runner approached on my left. *Oh, no way in hell.* We were neck and neck. Our strides were in sync, as if a reflection in a mirror. She was the only thing standing between me and my dream.

The first two runners crossed the finish line to earsplitting cheers from the crowd.

I willed myself to the end, pushing my body to its breaking point. In that final second, I threw my chest across the finish line and hoped to God I'd beaten her.

I ran until I was able to stop and bent at the waist, grasping my knees and gasping for air. Sweat glazed my eyes. My heartbeat ricocheted off my chest. It had been close. Too close for the human eye to detect. It would be a dead heat.

All I could do was wait. Wait for the photos to determine my fate.

I couldn't bear to look up into the crowd. I couldn't bear to see my parents, Logan, and Drew. I couldn't bear to see their faces if I'd finished fourth. I couldn't bear to let them see mine if I wasn't an Olympic medalist.

In the end, though, I knew I'd run my heart out. I'd given it my all. I'd done everything I was mentally and physically capable of doing. And if that wasn't good enough, then I didn't deserve to wear the medal.

I stood up with my hands grasping my soon-to-be cramping sides. My cheeks pulsed with heat and sweat drenched every part of my body as I walked in a small circle.

"Andi?"

That voice.

My head whipped around.

Drew hurried toward me, moving around coaches and runners. He threw his big arms around me and kissed me hard before pulling back to look at me. "You were amazing."

How was it that when my life, future, and dreams hung in the balance, he always showed up and made everything okay? I tried to smile, but I could feel my heartbeat pounding in my gums.

"You won. I just know you did." He released me and stepped back. "But no matter what happens, I still love you."

I cocked my head. "Seriously? Were you planning on dumping me if I didn't place?"

He cocked his own head, unfazed by my sarcasm.

As if it were happening in slow motion, Drew dropped down onto one knee in the middle of all the commotion and pulled a small black box from his pocket.

My eyes bugged out and my hands flew to my mouth. "Oh my God."

He looked up at me through those thick eyelashes and grinned. "Marry me, Andi. You're already the best thing that's ever happened to me. You challenge me. You push me. And above all, you love me. You're not my better half, you're my best half."

I stared down at this gorgeous, kind, compassionate guy who changed my world. Who changed himself to become the type of guy he thought I deserved. Who loved me more than anything else.

I dropped my hands. "It took you long enough."

His brows lifted. "Wasn't exactly the response I was hoping for."

I grinned. "Why, Drew? Why me?"

He flashed his cocky grin. It still made my stomach a fluttery mess. But this time it told me he remembered the question I'd asked him four years before. The one that explained his unwavering feelings for me, even after our rocky and unconventional start. "We crazy people need to stick together."

With a wide smile and absolutely no doubt in my mind that this was my fate—*he* was my fate, I nodded.

"I'm gonna need to hear you say it," he said.

As if the entire stadium didn't exist, I answered him. "Yes, Drew. I want to marry you. And have your football playing babies."

He threw back his head and laughed as he slipped the most beautiful cushion cut diamond ring onto my ring finger. The stone sparkled like crazy under the bright morning sun. Logan had been right about things that sparkled. They did make you happy.

A hush fell over the crowd as an Italian announcer's thickly accented voice projected through the speakers, reverberating throughout the stadium. "The third place finish goes to the United States' Andi Parker."

I closed my eyes and my head fell back. Pure bliss swept over me. Drew jumped up and grabbed me in his arms, spinning me around like I weighed nothing at all. "You did it, Andi! You won the medal!"

My eyelids slid back, only to find Drew's big bright eyes staring back at me. "*We* did it. We won the medal."

He didn't hesitate. His lips collided with mine. And in front of thousands of fans in that stadium and millions at home, we sucked some serious face. And I didn't care. I was engaged to someone who loved me more than life itself, and I just won the freaking bronze medal at the Olympics.

Euphoria I'd never experienced before gushed through every part of my body. If I didn't know any better, I would've thought I'd drift off and float away.

Eventually, I was pulled away from Drew and whisked off to be interviewed. The first reporter asked what I'd learned during my journey to the Olympics.

I leaned down, speaking into the cluster of microphones on the table in front of me. "I've learned two invaluable lessons over the past four years. First, without strife, there'd be no push to persevere. And without perseverance, there'd be no joy in success. And second..." I smiled into the camera, visualizing Drew's cocky grin on the other side. "Sometimes, if you dream big enough, all your dreams really do come true."

STAY TUNED FOR

Avery and Logan's story

After Avery
A novella

ACKNOWLEDGEMENTS

Thank you to the wonderful readers who made this second book possible. Had you not read, reviewed, and spread the word about *Until Alex*, I would not have had the courage to try again with *Since Drew*. Nothing, besides my family and friends, makes me happier than creating these fictional stories and characters. So thank you for making my dream come true!

Thank you to my husband for "patiently" tolerating my computer in front of me at all times. I appreciated your offer to be the cover model...Maybe next time. Thank you to my amazing little boy for bringing such happiness into my life (and still napping so I have time to write).

Thank you to my parents, sister, brother-in-law, family, and friends, for telling every person you come in contact with that I wrote a book. As embarrassing as it can be at times, I appreciate your support. You've motivated me to make this second novel even better knowing my first grade teacher or next door neighbor may soon have it in their hands. So thanks for that. I think...

Thank you to Letitia at RBA Designs for the beautiful cover. You were so wonderful to work with and captured exactly what I'd envisioned—bringing Drew very much to life.

Thank you, yet again, to my wonderful editor, author Stephanie Elliot, for your amazing editing and suggestions. Without you, I never would have begun this exciting journey. Please know I take full responsibility for any errors in this final draft since I've revised it at least twenty times since you read it—being the crazy reviser that I am.

Thank you to author Sierra Hill for helping with the blurb. You have such a beautiful way with words and helped me tremendously when I was stressing out. I'm so happy to have another author friend to share experiences with.

And lastly, thank you to Dali at TJ Loves to Read for beta reading. I truly appreciated you taking the time to help me. You gave me so many fantastic suggestions. It was exactly what I needed. You're the best!

ABOUT THE AUTHOR

J. Nathan resides on the east coast with her husband and son. She is an avid reader of all things romance. Happy endings are a must. Alpha males with chips on their shoulders are an added bonus. When she's not curled up with a good book, she can be found spending time with family and friends, teaching high school English, and working on her next novel.

CONTACT INFO

I love hearing from readers, so feel free to reach out to me at any of the links below.
Jnathan.net
https://www.goodreads.com/jnathan
https://www.facebook.com/jnathanauthor
https://twitter.com/@Jnathanbooks
jnathanbooks@aol.com

**If you've yet to read *Until Alex*,
check out some reviews on
Amazon and Goodreads.**

Made in the USA
Middletown, DE
21 April 2016